MYSTERY TIMES 2015

Other books in this series

Mystery Times Ten 2011
Mystery Times Nine 2012
Mystery Times 2013

MYSTERY TIMES 2015

With Stories by

Maddi Davidson • Linda S. Browning

Kim Kash • Georgia Ruth

Kate Fellowes • Selaine Henriksen

Elaine Menge • David Steven Rappoport

Edited by MaryChris Bradley

Buddhapuss Ink   Edison, NJ

Cover and Book Layout/Design © 2015 The Book Team
Editor, MaryChris Bradley
Copyeditor, Andrea H. Curley
Library of Congress Control Number: 2015955452
ISBN 978-1-941523-08-7 (Paperback Original)
First Printing December 2015

Foreword

WELCOME TO the 2015 edition of Mystery Times. The stories in this book were selected by our panels of readers and judges from more than one hundred and fifty entries. The top twenty went on to our Editorial Panel, who chose the final eight. Our goal: to celebrate the stories that our readers picked as the best.

To our judges: we couldn't have done this without you. You were amazing, churning through what seemed to be an endless stack of submissions; you were persistent, demanding, and dead-on in your picks. Thanks!

To our entrants: we offer a grateful thank-you for joining in the fun. We enjoyed reading your stories. We laughed; we cried; we were impressed by the quality of your writing. Way to go!

And to you, our readers: we hope you find this year's picks as entertaining as we have. We gave special notice to the top three winners, but we love them all. Thanks for choosing our humble book. Now, find a comfortable chair in a well-lit corner and prepare yourself; you're in for a treat!

MaryChris Bradley
Publisher, Buddhapuss Ink LLC

Contents

First Place: Heartfelt, Maddi Davidson   1

Second Place: Parlor Game, Linda S. Browning   15

Third Place: Pesticides Can Kill You, Kim Kash   37

Wheels of Fortune, Georgia Ruth   47

Stranger at the Door, Kate Fellowes   61

A Prescription for Murder, Selaine Henriksen   71

Requiem for a Hit Man, Elaine Menge   83

Leftovers, David Steven Rappoport   99

First Place

Heartfelt

Maddi Davidson

HANNAH FELT the chill of the mid-February day: cold, dreary, and the kind of damp that made your bones hurt if you were old enough. Today she felt old enough and then some. Bob lay on the frost-nipped grass, gasping for air and periodically flopping about as spasms gripped his chest.

He looks like a freshly landed fish, she thought. *Funny, I've always pictured him as a snake. But now? Decidedly a fat trout. A catch-and-throw-back trout.*

The cacophony of sirens reached a crescendo as a fire truck and ambulance rounded the corner and screeched in stereo down the street.

She wondered why they always sent a fire truck with an ambulance; she'd told them specifically it was a heart attack. Nothing on fire here: Bob's heart had been stone-cold for years.

Two men in dark-blue jackets with reflective EMT logos on the back jumped out of the ambulance and sprinted to Bob's side while neighbors popped their heads out of half-opened doors to discover the source of the hubbub. Most gave in to curiosity, venturing forth from their sepia-toned ranch homes to join the flock gathering across the street from the emergency vehicles.

Intent on watching the medics working on Bob, Hannah was barely aware that a man from the fire truck had approached her. It wasn't until he spoke that she realized he was there.

"What happened?"

Hannah turned to find baby-blue eyes staring at her. *Innocent eyes*, she thought. She blinked for a few moments, considering his question. Shit happens. Thirteen years of it.

"He came over. We fought. He stormed out and had a heart attack."

"Are you sure it was a heart attack?" he inquired.

I'd bet his life on it, she thought. "He has heart problems."

Baby-Blue Eyes nodded, asked if she was all right for now, then moved on and conferred with the medics as they ministered to Bob. A few moments later the medics loaded Bob on a gurney and wheeled him to the ambulance. Even after the ambulance had departed, barreling down the street, lights flashing and siren wailing, Hannah's neighbors remained clustered next to the fire truck like pigeons in hopes of a handout.

Baby-Blue Eyes returned to ask Hannah for more information about Bob. She responded to his questions while gazing at the spot near the curb where Bob had fallen. The warmth of his prostrate body had melted the frost, leaving a sodden brown mat of rye grass. *I'll plant something there this spring,* she thought, something symbolic. *Nightshade would be lovely, but it won't grow this far north. Maybe hemlock. Yes, hemlock would do nicely.*

Solicitously, the fireman inquired whether he should call someone to stay with her.

"Thank you," she said, "but no. Bob was my ex-husband, you see." Without speaking another word or acknowledging the congregation of neighbors, she turned and in short, rapid steps walked back to the house.

Hannah closed the front door behind her and leaned against it, her shoulders slumping. She viewed the wreckage of her living room and sighed deeply. Bob always threw things when he got angry, and she was fortunate not to be one of the things he threw this time. Ironic though that he'd managed to kill himself in this last barrage of vitriol.

First I'll call Asenka, she thought. Bob's barely legal-age, mail-order bride deserved to know that Bob would not be home for Valentine's Day. *Then I'll clean up this mess and take the busted equipment to a Dumpster. After that I'll pour myself a tall glass of the Veuve Clicquot I've been saving for just such a noteworthy occasion and take a nice bubble bath. An exceptionally nice bubble bath. Oh yes.*

Barely disguising her acute boredom and resentment, Amelia Jackson slumped in her black leather chair, taking notes as the speakers droned on. Amelia concentrated on not pursing her lips or playing with her hair and vigorously suppressed even the barest hint of an eye roll as she wondered if it was time to look for a new job.

Once Amelia was a rising star with the FBI, but her career had fallen off a cliff after a string of unfortunate events that had begun eleven months ago. A suspect had led her on a twenty-minute chase culminating at the San Diego Zoo, where he attempted to lose her by dodging through exotic fauna. She hadn't even been the one to fire the first half-dozen shots, as she noted for anybody and everybody who brought up the subject. Nevertheless, the bureau held her at fault for the giraffe's permanent limp and the female baboon whose large, flaming rear end—essential for luring males—needed plastic surgery. The last straw, or grain of rice, was when the government of China, with frosty formality, demanded the return of Zhou-Zhou the panda, who had developed noise induced panic attacks.

As a result of the Fractured Fauna Fiasco, as it was known across the bureau, Amelia had been transferred out of San Diego to the Salt Lake City office: purgatory for screw-up agents. It soon became apparent that her bad-karma fairy had transferred with her. First, there was the incident when she was tailing a suspected drug dealer. Tearing a fender off the governor's limo could happen to anybody, really. That was followed by the disaster involving a credit card fraud ring of celebrity look-alikes. She'd caught a perp in the act of ringing up an enormous bill: he was, she said triumphantly as she slapped on the cuffs, at best a third-rate copy of George Clooney. Alas, he turned out to be the original item. The heinous PR reverberated for weeks. Amelia received a plethora of anonymous LOL e-mails, which, she came to understand, stood for lampooned on Leno.

Like a supernova, her rising star had collapsed into a black hole, to the point that she no longer was given the CCCPs (cool, career-climbing projects) but assigned to all the SLJs (shitty little jobs). The most recent one had brought her to this meeting in Bozeman, Montana, with Heartek Devices, a medical equipment firm. She glanced out the conference room window: mid-May and it was snowing. God, she wished she were back in San Diego, or any place that didn't sell makeup, ammunition, and bait in the same store.

Heartek's president, Mark Weiner, a spare, ascetic fifty-year-old, babbled incessantly about the fly fishing in Bozeman within minutes of introductions. She nearly choked when he mentioned olive stimulators, which sounded to her more like a cocktail hour sex toy than a fishing lure. During his laborious PowerPoint presentation, Amelia had learned way more than she ever wanted to know about ICDs—implantable cardiac defibrillators—in general, and the HT200 model in particular. She could have done without the stomach-churning photos of an implant operation. Two cups of distilled-over-three-hours coffee hadn't helped.

According to Heartek, a Boise hospital suspected an HT200 model of malfunctioning by delivering repeated high-voltage shocks to the chest of a forty-two-year-old male, now deceased. One could say he was overpowered. A hospital doctor had removed the ICD from the victim's chest and returned it to Heartek for evaluation. The vice president of design, Carl Hudge (shaved head, black, thick-rimmed glasses, the droning monotone of an engineer entranced by all things electronic), enumerated in excruciating detail the series of tests Heartek had conducted on the device. Furthermore, Heartek had sent a team to check the hospital's programmer: not a geek for hire but a laptop-sized device used to monitor and adjust the implant by sending instructions wirelessly. Furthermore, two of Heartek's scientists visited the site of the man's death to determine if electromagnetic interference in the area could have caused the ICD malfunction. She mentally translated their assertion of "no stone left unturned" to "no ass left uncovered."

"So you see," Mark Weiner said, speaking earnestly as the last of the PowerPoint slides flashed on the screen, "we've checked everything thoroughly and found nothing wrong. The hospital assures us that there was no unauthorized access to their programmer. The only plausible explanation, therefore, is that the ICD was hacked. Someone constructed a device that could reprogram the HT200 to deliver a string of deadly shocks."

All of which constituted a rehash of the theory Heartek had been pushing with the FBI for several weeks. The bureau didn't buy it. "I've been hacked" is the twenty-first-century equivalent of "the dog ate my homework" on the lame-excuse-o-meter, not to mention that mechanical murder wasn't normally the FBI's remit. After threats from Heartek to notify their senator, the FBI decided to send Amelia for a face-to-face meeting with the company. Her job was to listen attentively and then tell Heartek in a respectful manner but in words of one syllable to cease and desist their badgering. They'd get a hearing, but the answer was foreordained: the FBI is not interested.

Amelia sat up straight in her chair, ready to do her duty. "Interesting theory," she said, "but even in the unlikely event the defibrillator was hacked—"

"It *was* hacked," Hudge said.

"Whatever. I mean, of course, whatever the case," Amelia said, "it's a local matter. The FBI only investigates cyber crimes that are significant. This man's death hardly counts as significant, except, of course, to his loved ones."

Hudge leaned forward in his chair. "Don't you understand? This is the first time one of these devices has ever been hacked. We've got a couple hundred thousand of these implanted in patients. What if the perpetrator gets his jollies killing people and decides to sell his services on the Internet? Would the EFF BEE EYE see, I dunno, a medical-murder-for-hire-dot-com site as significant?"

Amelia stiffened at the sarcasm. "If your defibrillators are so prone to hacking," she said, "perhaps you should consider upgrading your software." She stopped herself from adding, "and consider hiring a really good product liability attorney."

Hudge glared at her, but it was Mark Weiner who spoke, his jaw clenching. "We've looked into making the older devices more secure. We can't do it just by upgrading the software; we'd need to implant more hardware in each patient's chest. And since the ICDs of our competitors function along similar lines, that could mean upward of one million patients worldwide undergoing surgery."

Amelia was stunned. A million chests cut open, buckets of blood. Not a pretty thought, or a beauteous sight. "Maybe you should wait to see if there are any other attacks before—"

"Absolutely not," Weiner said, now clearly angry. "If the FBI isn't going to take this seriously, we'll escalate; the senior senator from Montana, John Swaggert, lives right here in Bozeman. You might have heard of him; he's the chairman of the Senate Judiciary Committee, which has oversight of the FBI."

"Yes, I know," Amelia said. Senator Swaggert was famous in the bureau for his keen interest in the FBI's budget. This assignment was turning into a disaster—as if she needed another one.

"Do we need to give Senator Swaggert a call?" Weiner said.

Amelia knew when she was beaten. Though they'd probably say whupped here in Montana.

One very long phone call later, her boss gave the go-ahead to investigate, adding, "I have every confidence in your abilities." What he really meant was "It's a waste of FBI time, but do enough to placate Heartek and keep Swaggert out of the picture." And, of course, "Don't screw it up."

Amelia spent five days in Boise investigating Bob Cheatham's background to determine why someone might want to kill him. Court records and interviews with his ex-wife, neighbors, and colleagues revealed a guy with a greased zipper who was little missed, especially by his conquests.

Seducing a mother and daughter—Krissy and Kaycie Leckie—had been the nadir of Bob's narcissistic pursuits and the proximate cause of his divorce. He'd sent mother and daughter identical valentines but had mixed up the cards and envelopes. Separately (because they weren't speaking to each other), Krissy and Kaycie had tracked down Bob's wife, Hannah, to let her know just what a no-good, low-down cockroach of a husband she had. Three potential perps right there, although Krissy and Kaycie, who were avid deer hunters, seemed more the type who would track the varmint down and stick his head on the wall. And Hannah had come across as sweet but not very competent.

Even the widow, Asenka, a barely twenty-year-old Russian courted by the deceased via e-mail, betrothed, and married to Bob within four months of his divorce, didn't seem particularly interested in talking about her dead husband. She did, however, enthuse about her puppy, Vladimir, of indeterminate breed, acquired since her husband's death. "I had him, how you say, 'feexed'? Bob needed zat, I theenk."

There was no shortage of women with ready motive and even readier weaponry, Idaho being a right-to-carry state, but Amelia had yet to locate one with a sufficient geek quotient to be considered a suspect. Hudge had explained to her that building a hacking device required "USRP and software like GNU Radio, TTJY, and Mosic."

Amelia had stifled her impulse to add, "EIEIO."

Continuing her due diligence, Amelia set aside a day to interview the hospital cardiac-care staff. Dr. Bird, the head of the cardiac unit, radiated a no-nonsense professionalism when discussing hospital procedures and sat behind a large desk on which she had amassed stacks of folders.

"Bob Cheatham came in twice a year for his unit to be checked," Dr. Bird said.

Amelia was unsuccessful in suppressing a laugh.

"I meant, of course, his *defibrillator*." The doctor looked over her trifocals disapprovingly before refocusing her attention on the patient history folder. "During Mr. Cheatham's last visit, four months ago, we determined there had been no significant change in episodes of arrhythmia, and the unit was operating correctly. After his death we reviewed the electronic record maintained by the ICD and discovered that in the days leading up to his death, there were three distinct episodes of the ICD delivering a high-voltage shock. Strangely, these occurred at approximately the same time on successive days."

"When was that?" Amelia leaned forward in her seat.

"Between noon and one, the lunch hour. Each shock exceeded 750 volts." She looked up from her notes. "A shock of that magnitude causes significant chest pain. We tell our patients to call us immediately when that happens. Why Mr. Cheatham didn't, I don't know." She returned to her notes. "On the day of his death, the defibrillator delivered a series of 750- to 800-volt shocks beginning at 1:38 P.M. The defib continued to deliver shocks until it was disconnected, well after he was dead."

"And you think a malfunction caused this?"

"Yes. There is no record of severe arrhythmia that would have triggered the ICD to operate in such a manner."

"But three days in a row at the same time?"

Dr. Bird shrugged. "He could have been near a magnetic field or area of intense electrical activity, which caused the unit to misfire. If he ate lunch at the same place each day, that would explain the timing coincidence. Perhaps Cheatham recognized this and had lunch at a different locale on the fourth day. However, exposure to the magnetic field and high level of electrical activity may have caused a malfunction in the unit, which manifested itself in the series of uncontrolled shocks that caused Cheatham's death."

"What about a theory that includes someone from the hospital deliberately delivering those shocks?"

Dr. Bird shook her head. "The programmer, that's the small computer used to communicate with the ICD, operates wirelessly, but it needs to be within fifteen or twenty feet of the ICD."

Amelia nodded her head.

"None of our programmers ever leave the hospital; nor does anyone in my group have a motive to harm Mr. Cheatham."

"What about someone else in the hospital?"

Dr. Bird shook her head.

"Doctor, staff, volunteer, maintenance staff?"

Dr. Bird's expression changed. She tapped her finger nervously on the desk.

"You've thought of someone," Amelia said.

"Maybe," Dr. Bird responded. "Bob's ex-wife, Hannah Cheatham, is a volunteer at the hospital. She's worked in this department a few times. Clerical work mostly: filing, copying, memos, that sort of thing. But I will not, cannot, believe it of her."

Amelia looked triumphant.

Dr. Bird continued. "Hannah and I are in the same Bible study at Calvary Presbyterian. She's a lovely person. Bob, on the other hand, was a slime bag of the worst kind."

"'Cockroach' has been a popular descriptor."

"Those are dispatched far more easily. If he'd been my husband, I would have kicked his crotch a few times and sent him packing." She shook her head. "Hannah would not kill Bob, even if she had the know-how, and that's a big *if*. Hannah never progressed further than a few courses in community college before she met and married Bob."

Amelia pursued the issue, asking about duplicate programming devices. "Impossible," she was told. Programmers were never sold to individuals. Even with access to a programmer, one would need the correct model plus confidential information about the patient to be able to administer shocks.

Dr. Bird's staff told similar stories. When Amelia asked whether

Hannah could have learned how to operate a programmer, they laughed in her face. Hannah was kind and well-meaning and could follow simple instructions, but wasn't very bright. Certainly not intelligent enough to plan a high-tech murder.

"Sorry to bother you, but I have a few more questions."

Hannah wondered why the female FBI agent was back on her doorstep huddling under a black umbrella while a thunderstorm raged outside. Hannah beckoned her in. At least the agent had the good manners to shake her umbrella outside before entering, and to wipe her feet. Even though the blue carpet had worn patches, and the curtains and upholstery were faded, Hannah was proud of her home, which she kept neat and clean.

Hannah observed Amelia eyeing the fresh pink hydrangeas that she had placed in a simple crockery jug on a small table.

"Weren't those blue when I was here Tuesday?" Amelia said.

"New flowers. I love hydrangeas: their shape, their beautiful color. I've been thinking of planting a few in my new garden in front, next to the curb."

Amelia moved toward the table and began fingering the flowers. "My aunt Mary loved flower arranging and tried to teach me the basics of scale, texture, spacing, and form. She liked explaining the meanings of certain flowers and how they could be arranged to send a message."

Hannah forced herself to smile. "How interesting. Did your aunt tell you that flowers can have multiple meanings?"

The house lit up as lightning flashed outside, followed by a long roll of thunder. Amelia waited for the rumble to pass before speaking. "She did. As I recall, hydrangeas symbolize boastfulness, or sincerely heartfelt, or... what was it? Oh yes, a cold heart." Amelia paused. "What do they signify for you?"

"Thankfulness for my good life."

Before Amelia could say more, Hannah asked her to take a seat while she prepared a snack.

Hannah emerged from the kitchen a few minutes later with two tall glasses, a pitcher of lemonade, and a plate of assorted cookies on a tray. Amelia was seated on one of the faded-green wing chairs and began speaking as Hannah poured the lemonade.

"You're my last interview before I return to Salt Lake. I thought you might like to know my findings."

"Yes, I would." Hannah handed Amelia her glass as lightning again lit up the house, this time followed by a sharp crack.

"Your friends have confirmed what you told me about Bob."

"That he was lower than a snake's belly?"

Amelia nodded. "That he beat you and put you in the hospital several times when you were married and that he cheated on you."

"I told you; he made my life miserable. That's why we divorced. I admit I'm not sorry he's dead. Now that I'm finally and truly free of him, I plan to celebrate."

"I've also learned that before his death, Bob's device malfunctioned several times, yet he didn't report it to the hospital."

Hannah shrugged. "I wouldn't know about that." About the not going to the hospital. She knew about the malfunctions.

"There's only one theory that makes sense," Amelia said.

Hannah flinched at the sharp boom outside. That was close.

Amelia continued. "I believe that you followed Mr. Cheatham during his lunch hour three days in a row and used an ICD programmer to shock his heart. The fourth day you didn't show up, and he didn't have an attack. He made the connection and came here to confront you. What happened next? Did he hit you? Start to beat you? Did you then shock him to stop the beating? You know that if you delivered the fatal shocks because you feared for your life, it could be considered self-defense."

Hannah took a long drink of her lemonade and then nibbled on the edge of a sugar cookie. "I don't have an ICD programmer." Not since she took it apart, drove to Mountain View, and deposited the pieces in a Dumpster at night. She was fairly sure she hadn't been seen.

"And I didn't kill him." Just given him a few jolts as payback for the pain he caused for so many years. But when he had stormed into her house, discovered her programmer, and thrown it against the wall, he must have jammed the emergency shock button. It wouldn't turn off. She'd tried to switch it off. Really, she had.

Amelia sat back in the wing chair. "The hospital told me that ICD programmers cannot be sold to individuals, but I found used ones available on eBay. A little digging and I expect I could discover that an HT200 was sold to someone in the Boise area."

Hannah smiled but said nothing. She didn't know about Boise, but an eminently forgettable, careworn woman had picked one up at a PO box in Bend, Oregon, registered to a fake health care company.

"Did you know that the manuals for how to use the HT200 are on the Internet?" Amelia said.

"Doesn't that mean anyone could have done it?" Hannah replied. It had been a lovely drive to Seattle, where she had used the public library computers. Their wireless networks were much faster when you were downloading large, complex documentation.

"Not quite. The killer would need the specific model number of Mr. Cheatham's implant and the hospital's assigned patient number, which was used as an access password."

"A hospital employee, then."

"Like you," Amelia said.

The two women looked at each other.

"Are you arresting me for a crime?"

"I will be."

Hannah looked away, hoping her eyes didn't betray her despair, and was surprised to see sunshine streaming through the window.

"No?" Amelia was stunned.

"No," responded Robert Barkeley, special agent in charge of the Salt Lake City office. "I confirmed it with headquarters. We will not take this any further."

"Why the hell not?" Amelia said. She'd done a darn good job on a dog of an assignment, and for what?

"Think about it. The government will have to prove how easy it was for Hannah Cheatham to hack her ex-husband's ICD. A few minutes on eBay to find and order a device, a quick download of the manuals from the Internet and she had her loaded gun, so to speak. If that news leaked—and it will—there are many unhappy women like Hannah who would be able to dispose of their husbands with SMOP."

"Beg pardon?" Amelia said.

"A simple matter of programming."

"They would need the hospital ID number."

"Prominently displayed on hospital bills."

"Circumstantial evidence would point to them. They'd be caught."

"Like Hannah? We both know there isn't enough evidence to convict her. A would-be killer could repeatedly zap her victim until he died and then call 911. It's the perfect copycat crime."

"We're letting Hannah Cheatham get away with murder?"

"Just this one."

"And what about Heartek's concerns and their threat to get Senator Swaggert involved?"

"Don't worry. Someone higher up the ladder will deal with the senator."

Amelia dropped her head, thinking.

"The decision is final," Barkeley said, sensing another objection might be forthcoming.

"Well then," Amelia said, raising her head, "may I ask you another question?"

"Not about this case."

"Oh, it's not." Amelia gave a small, insightful smile. "It's just that I heard a rumor that the director of the FBI is going through a messy divorce right now. Is that right?"

"Where did you hear that?"

"I know a few people in DC. I heard or read that the director had an ICD implanted last year."

Barkeley was quiet as he stared at Amelia. She met his gaze steadily.

"Maybe you should be rewarded for your good work on this case," he said.

Amelia's smile grew larger. "You know, I think I could be much more effective in the San Diego office."

Two weeks later, Hannah Cheatham was astonished when the florist delivered a dozen roses in a large, heart-shaped vase.

She removed the wilting hydrangeas and placed the new arrangement on her dining-room table before opening a small envelope and reading the card within.

As she dropped the card in the trash, she spoke softly to herself. "And here I had no idea that dark-pink roses were a symbol of gratitude."

AUTHOR

MADDI DAVIDSON is the pen name for two sisters, Mary Ann Davidson and Diane Davidson, who are giving each other high-fives over their story appearing in *Mystery Times 2015*. Residing on opposite coasts of the US, the sisters have spent too many years inflicting "new and improved" information technology on leery users. In addition to writing short stories, they've published three novels in the Miss-Information Technology Mystery Series, available through Amazon: *Outsourcing Murder*, *Denial of Service*, and *With Murder You Get Sushi*. More information about Maddi is available on their website: maddidavidson.com.

Second Place

Parlor Game

Linda S. Browning

AFTER ANGIE Moulton had married Brad, she became obsessed with my never-married state. Angie alleges I am the sole remaining single person from our graduating class at UT. She has no University of Tennessee statistics to support this claim, but claim it she does.

I *was* engaged for about thirty minutes when I was twenty-seven, but I couldn't take the pressure. I, Olivia Jane Honeycutt, am doing just fine as a single entity. I make a good living as a journalist. I keep myself in shape and rarely allow my five-foot-two frame to exceed 120 pounds. I wear my light-brown hair (with honey-blond, sun/salon-kissed highlights) shoulder length. I date occasionally.

I migrated to Nashville after graduation. Angie lives in Knoxville with Brad.

We get together every few months for a girls' weekend. She arrived at my townhome late Friday night. Angie likes to go yard saling. I am not impressed by the junk of other people. However, I agreed to spend Saturday yard saling with my friend. It being early summer, the darned things were everywhere. We went to the Hendersonville area of Nashville, where the moneyed folk live. Poking through some stuff on a table I uncovered a Ouija board. Memories of slumber parties in the late eighties wafted through my head: little girls littered across a living-room floor trying to conjure up dead people. All of us were around ten years old and didn't know many dead people. So we attempted to contact the usual dead suspects: Marilyn Monroe, John Lennon, President Kennedy, and anyone else we were pretty sure was dead.

I bought it on a whim for fifty cents. Relaxing with some wine that evening, I challenged Angie to a game. "Want to play with the Ouija board? Or are you sc-car-ed?"

"Do you have the rules?"

"Didn't you ever play with a Ouija board as a kid?"

"Yeah, a few times."

"So, all we do is place a finger or two on the pointer thingy and tell the board we want to talk to a dead person."

"I don't wish to speak to any dead people."

"Okay. Ask the board a question about the future or the past. C'mon, I dare you!"

"Liv, if you had a social life, you wouldn't be playing kid games on a Saturday night."

"Do you want to play or not?"

"Okay."

I placed the board on the coffee table, and Angie and I sat on the floor facing each other. The board was identical to the one I remembered from childhood. A picture of the sun in the upper left-hand corner with the word YES stenciled beside it. An image of the moon in the top right corner with the word NO stenciled beside it. Centered between the sun and the moon at the top of the board was the name Ouija, The Mystifying Oracle. In the middle of the board, the letters A through M were printed in an upside down smile with the letters N through Z directly beneath. In a horizontal line beneath the letters appeared the numbers 1 2 3 4 5 6 7 8 9 0. The word GOODBYE was centered at the bottom of the board. The heart-shaped indicator had a clear plastic lens near the pointy end.

"Put one finger lightly on the pointer thingy on your side."

She did as instructed, and I gently placed my index finger on the other side.

"Is anybody out there?" she asked melodramatically.

I jerked my hand away. "If we ask the cosmos in general, we risk inviting an evil ghost or a demon."

"Girl, you need a life so baaaaad." She laughed. "Let's ask the board something about today, as a test."

"Okay."

With poised fingertips Angie asked, "Where did Liv buy this game today?"

The pointer thingy quickly moved from letter to letter.

POWDERRUN

We looked at one another with raised eyebrows.

I shrugged. "We went to four sales on Powell Street."

The indicator skipped down to the numbers and then back up to the letters.

2496NORTHPOWDERRUN

Angie stretched out her arm to snag her purse from beside the sofa. Removing the newspaper with the circled yard sales, she peered over her reading glasses. "Which yard sale did you buy this at?"

"The second one."

She licked a finger and gave the air an imaginary swipe. "2496 North Powder Run. Score one for the magic board!"

Fingers in place, Angie asked, "Are you dead?"

The indicator skated across the face of the board.

YES

"Did you once live at that address?" I asked.

When nothing happened, I started, "That doesn't tell us..." Before I could finish my thought, the indicator swayed drunkenly away from the word, and then slammed back emphatically.

YES

Angie whispered, "I guess that's a yes. How old were you when you died?"

15

"You were fifteen?" I confirmed.

YES

"What was your name?"

The indicator flew from letter to letter.

SOPHIEMATHEWS

I sounded it out and muttered, "Sophie Mathews."

"I want to stop playing, Liv." Angie dropped her hand. The plastic zoomed beneath my finger.

NO

"You're doing that. I'm not even touching it."

"How did you die?" I whispered.

Nothing. No movement. I began to feel odd. My breathing became fast and shallow.

Angie ordered, "Stop clowning around."

I wasn't clowning. I couldn't breathe. My hands flew to my throat.

"Oh my God, Liv!" She jumped to her feet, ran around the coffee table, and started thumping on my back.

I couldn't draw even the tiniest breath. I clawed at my throat. The tightness eased. I guzzled air.

Angie pointed a shaky finger at me, gasping, "Lo-ook at your throat! Did you do that?"

I struggled to my feet and stumbled into the hall bathroom. We stood side by side staring in the mirror at the horrific crimson marks encircling my throat.

She led me to the bedroom and helped me to lie down. "I'll get you some water."

I closed my eyes and inhaled cautiously.

Angie hustled back into the bedroom and handed me a glass of water. Sitting on the bed beside me, she exclaimed, "They're gone!"

"What?" I sputtered into the glass.

"The marks on your neck are gone!"

Angie brought me a hand mirror. She was right.

We spent the remainder of the evening telling each other we had overreacted. As Angie was preparing to get on the road back to Knoxville the next morning, she asked, "You're sure you're okay this morning, Liv?"

"Yes, I'm all right." I gave her a hug.

After Angie left, I went upstairs with the intention of taking a long shower. I started shedding clothes as I entered the bedroom and crossed to the bed where I routinely tossed a ratty old bathrobe. I stared down at the Ouija board sitting there with the pointer thingy sitting on top. I was positive I had left it in the kitchen.

Angie must have put it here as a joke.

I retrieved the board and pointer thingy and set them on the dresser. I closed myself in the bathroom with only the hot water and steam for company. Returning the bedroom I yelped to find the Ouija board and pointer thingy on the bed, *again*.

"That's it, you're going in the trash."

The pointer thingy crawled across the board.

NO

You're a journalist. The first thing you do with any story is research.
Dressing in jeans and a t-shirt, I padded downstairs in my bare

feet with the accursed board tucked under my arm. I laid it on the kitchen table next to my laptop and opened up a search engine. I typed "Ouija Board" into the search line.

> The Ouija board was introduced in 1890 by Elijah Bond as a harmless parlor game and was not associated with the occult until World War I. Pearl Curran, a St. Louis housewife, allegedly made contact with a spirit by the name of Patience Worth, who claimed to have been killed by American Indians after coming to America in the mid 1600s.

I learned that the so-called unconscious movements of the pointer had been explained by scientists as a psychophysiological phenomenon known as the "ideomotor" effect. That the key person operating the pointer is driving the conversation without conscious awareness.

That didn't explain why I almost choked to death, or how the pointer had moved without my touching it. I pushed all thoughts of the Ouija and Sophie Mathews from my mind and spent the remainder of the day puttering around the house. Toward evening I read a nonsense/action novel by one of my favorite authors until I got sleepy. Around midnight I turned off the bedside light and drifted off. I don't know how long I had been asleep before I started to dream.

> *It was summer, and I was walking beside a calm lake. I was alone, but there was a low rumble of voices only a short distance away. I was meeting someone. I was nervous and excited.*
>
> *The dream staggered forward.*
>
> *I was walking beside the lake again. I was returning from my rendezvous; my stomach fluttered with new and welcomed sensations.*
>
> *The dream staggered forward.*
>
> *A large man loomed above me. I opened my mouth to scream. He lifted me off my feet with two hands around my throat; successfully cutting off my cries. I struggled and clawed at his face. Dangling from his fists like a caught fish, he carried me into the lake until I was neck deep. He plunged my head beneath the water and loosened the grip on my throat. My lungs flooded. It*

was a short dream. My murder hadn't taken long at all.

I awoke clawing and gasping for air. Scrubbing both eyes with my fists, I stood and took unsteady steps toward the bathroom. My bare feet hit wet carpeting. After turning on the bedside lamp, I realized I had knocked over the water glass I keep next to the bed. The almost-empty glass lay on its side, water plopping to the carpet. I made my way to the bathroom with the intention of washing my face and getting a towel to mop up the water. Turning on the bathroom light, I leaned heavily against the vanity and looked in the mirror.

She was behind me. She was a couple of inches taller than me and really skinny. She had very long, dark hair, parted down the middle like the singer Cher when she was with Sonny. She wore cut-off blue jeans frayed at the hem and a pink-and-white striped short-sleeved blouse. She had on shiny pink lip gloss. There was a feathery whisper of movement against my hair as I watched her arm float over my shoulder. Her short nails were painted to match her lip gloss. She touched a finger to her mirrored self: Peter Pan trying to capture his shadow. There was no malevolence in this apparition, only an abundance of wanting. She met my eyes for the briefest of moments. Her lips formed a weary, weak smile.

The only face in the mirror was my own. Sophie Mathews was gone. Sinking to the cool ceramic tile, I hugged my knees and wept for this incomplete young woman. I accepted Sophie's ghostly visit without question. She was real.

I slept deeply, no more dreams. I woke up shortly after 6 A.M. and made my way to the kitchen and the coffeemaker. The Ouija board sat on the kitchen table beside my laptop. Fortified with coffee and a piece of toast, I settled at the table.

"Good morning, Sophie," I addressed the board.

The pointer sailed and settled on the sun.

Powering my laptop, I entered "Sophie Mathews" into a search engine mumbling, "When did you die, Sophie?" The pointer scratched across the board.

1966

I entered "Sophie Mathews/Nashville/1966"

15-year-old Sophie Mathews died June 14, 1966, while attending a party for a friend's sixteenth birthday at Hickory Lake State Park. Her boyfriend discovered her floating facedown near an area of the lake known as the Willows. The boy dragged her from the water and tried to revive her. She was pronounced dead at the scene. Another article a few days later listed her death as a homicide by drowning.

Turning to the Ouija, I touched the pointer gently. "What happened, Sophie?" After a few moments the pointer (whom I now thought of as Sophie) began to move in circles.

"Did your boyfriend kill you?"

NO

"Do you know who killed you?"

YES

"Did the police catch them?"

NO

"Who are they, Sophie? Give me a name?"

ROY

"Do you know Roy's last name?"

NO

"How did you know Roy?"

Sophie moved sluggishly in circles.

TIRED

"It must take a lot of psychic energy to talk with me." I cupped Sophie in my hand. She trembled beneath my fingers. She was crying.

"I will ask yes-or-no questions so you won't have to spell."

I asked a series of questions, and she answered each one.

Roy had not been her friend or acquaintance. When I asked whether he had been a family friend, she paced back and forth between the YES and NO destinations.

"Roy was somebody known by your family but not a friend?"

YES

"I'm going to contact the police and see what I can find out about your murder and this Roy guy. Is there anything else you want to tell me before I call them?"

MYRING

"Myring? Is that Roy's last name?"

NO

I verbalized, "Myring...myring...my." The pointer hopped once beneath my finger."

"Are you trying to tell me something about your ring?"

YES

"What about your ring?"

FACE

Then I got it. "You scratched his face with your ring?" I announced triumphantly, sounding like a contestant on *Wheel of Fortune*.

YES

Since the yard sale and Hickory Lake are both in the Hendersonville area, I called their local police department. I identified myself to the woman and explained that I needed to speak with someone about the murder of Sophie Mathews in 1966. After holding for a couple of minutes, the woman returned. "Can you meet with Detective Presley Warren here at the police department at 1 o'clock?" I agreed.

Not content to sit surfing the Web for bits and pieces on Sophie's murder, I decided to visit Hickory Lake State Park. Picking up my purse, I started toward the door into the garage. The pointer started clattering on the Ouija board. I walked over to the kitchen table and looked down at the board. Sophie scrawled TAKEME.

I stuffed the board and Sophie into a plastic grocery sack and headed to my car.

I discovered a picnic area and pavilion known as the Willows at Hickory Lake. It being Monday, there weren't many people around. I parked near the pavilion and opened my car door in preparation to exit. Sophie rustled the plastic sack. I reached across to the passenger seat and snagged the bag.

I crossed the grass to walk along the lake. After a few minutes, I rounded a bend. Looking behind me I noted that the pavilion was no longer in sight. I stopped beneath an enormous, lovely willow; a thick copse of trees was to my left. My stomach fluttered with fear and delight. The sensations lasted about five minutes. Languidly I turned to retrace my steps to the pavilion. After about ten steps the plastic sack started to shake violently, and I gripped it tightly. A riot of sensations danced through my body in quick succession: surprise, uneasiness, disgust, fear. Then anger—consuming anger. Invisible, murderous hands encircled my throat. My legs running in place,

I was propelled backward into the lake. Striking out at my unseen assailant, I dropped the plastic sack…and Sophie. I fell to my knees beside the trees. Gradually my breathing slowed. It was my dream—this had been Sophie's nightmare.

I went to the Hendersonville Police Department and told the officer at the front desk I had an appointment with Detective Presley Warren. A minute later a tall, good-looking man walked into the lobby area. I wished I had taken more care with my appearance. Approaching, he held out his hand to shake. "Miss Honeycutt, I am Detective Presley Warren. I'm told you are here about a cold case?"

"Yes. Sophie Mathews," I said, standing and shaking his hand. Good grip, nice eyes, tall—my internal dialog couldn't seem to shut up.

He offered me coffee, which I declined. He seated me at a small table and sat across from me. He flipped open a folder. "After you called I pulled the file. This murder was forty-seven years ago, Miss Honeycutt. I understand you are a journalist. Are you researching a story?"

I deflected. "Your mother was an Elvis fan but couldn't bring herself to name you Elvis. Am I right?"

He grinned and nodded I had guessed correctly.

"You're a journalist?" he persisted.

"Yes."

"Why are you here, Miss Honeycutt?"

"This case is forty-seven years old and unsolved. You don't have anything to lose by answering my questions. I won't write anything without it being vetted by you and your superiors." A journalist writing a story about a cold case was certainly more believable than connecting with a ghost via a Ouija board.

When he didn't say anything, I suggested, "How about this? I am going to make some statements about the case, and you tell me whether I have the facts correct or not."

"Okay." He nodded.

"Sophie Mathews was brutally strangled prior to being held beneath the waters of Hickory Lake."

He glanced at the record and with a slight widening of the eyes asked, "How did you know? Those facts were never revealed to the press or the public."

"In fact, Sophie was so violently strangled that the medical examiner determined she had been lifted off her feet by someone of immense strength. The force of the attack suggested the attacker was in a fury. What about evidence? Were there footprints? What about recovering fingerprints from her neck?"

Concentrating again on the paperwork before him, he said, "I'm not sure they could lift fingerprints from skin forty-seven years ago. Remember, she had been in the water."

"Not for very long."

"No, not for very long." He referred again to the report. "The victim was dating a boy by the name of Jake Thorne at the time. According to him, he and Sophie had agreed to slip away from the party and meet at a big willow tree beside the lake. The boy said they kissed and messed around. Thorne headed back to the party. Sophie was to follow a few minutes later. When she hadn't returned after fifteen minutes, the boy went looking for her. He found her in the water, dragged her out, and hollered for help. Every kid in the area trampled all over the crime scene. What is going on here, Miss Honeycutt?"

"Liv, please."

"Are you going to tell me what this is about, Liv?"

"Was there a boy or a man interviewed with the first name of Roy?"

"What is driving this meeting, Liv?"

"Do Sophie's parents still live in the area?" I continued.

"They are both deceased. There was an older brother."

"Yes. Brian Mathews." I had read his name in Sophie's obituary.

The plastic grocery sack in the chair next to me rustled.

"What is that noise?" He stared at the bag.

"Oh, I must have left my cell phone in the vibrate mode." I opened the plastic bag and rested my hand on the pointer. Sophie stilled.

"You keep your phone in a plastic sack?" he asked, one eyebrow raised.

"Yes…well, yes, I do."

Standing (gathering my purse and Sophie), I extended my hand across the table. "Thank you for your help, Detective."

He stood and shook my hand. "Please call me Presley. Look, I can't stop you from doing investigative research on a cold case, Liv, but keep me informed."

"Yes, I will."

I dropped his hand and opened the door to leave. My eyes went to his wedding ring finger. No ring. Before closing the door, I said, "Sophie was wearing a ring when she was attacked. She raked it across the face of her assailant. You need to find that ring. They didn't know about DNA in 1966." I left him standing beside the table.

Sophie and I stopped for Chinese takeout. Sitting at the kitchen table with the board, food, and Sophie near my hand, I said, "Why aren't you with your parents?"

HEARTHEM

"You hear them? Are they calling for you?"

YES

"Go to them."

CANT

"Why not?"

ROY

"I will get Roy for you. God wants you to be at peace, Sophie."

TIRED

"I'm a little tired myself."

We sat quietly for a while, and I poked around at my take-out food. "He has laugh wrinkles beside his eyes. He isn't as tough as he pretends to be. The detective, I mean."

YES

I checked the phone book for Brian Mathews and found eight listings. Sophie had no idea where to find her brother; however, she was positive that both Brian and this Roy person were still alive. We were trying to zoom in on identifying the Roy person with a series of yes-and-no questions when my doorbell rang. I left Sophie and the board on the table, and went to answer the door.

The peephole revealed the very good-looking Detective Warren. Opening the door, I opted for levity and demanded theatrically, "Do you have a warrant?"

His eyes and mouth smiled in response. "No. I would like to come in and talk to you in more depth about the 1966 case."

I invited him in, and he followed me to the kitchen. His eyes swept the contents of the table and the detritus of my Chinese takeout. He was doing his detective thing. I wished I had hidden the Ouija board. I picked up the board and set it on the counter along with the pointer (Sophie). I invited him to sit and offered something to drink, which he declined.

"How did you know my address?"

"I'm a detective."

"Ah."

"Are you married or dating anybody?"

I liked that…directness. "No to both questions," I answered just as directly. I raised my eyebrows. "You?"

"I was married for a couple of years. It didn't work out. No kids. Not dating currently."

"Okay…what else do we need to get out of the way? I'm thirty-four."

"Forty-one."

"Do you want to have sex now or later?" I deadpanned.

He laughed. I had been right about the laugh lines. He pivoted to the alleged reason for his visit. "So, how did you know about the strangulation attempt and the ring? It was a birthstone ring in the shape of a heart. Sophie Mathews was born in April; her birthstone was a diamond."

"Diamond?"

"Yes, but the ring wasn't worth a whole lot. The gems were little bitty diamond chips."

"Do you still have it in evidence? Maybe you can get the killer's DNA!"

"According to the record, the ring was returned to her parents."

"And they're dead."

"Yes."

"But Brian Mathews, her brother. He's not dead, is he? Maybe he still lives around here. He might have the ring!"

Instead of commenting on the whereabouts of Sophie's brother, he said flatly, "Roy Compton."

Sophie fell off the counter with a clatter. I jumped at least a foot. Before I could take a step to come to her aid, the board was swept to the floor by an unseen hand.

"Stop it, Sophie!" I yelled.

Presley's eyes got huge, and he barked, "What the hell just happened? How did you do that? Magnets? Wires? We've shut down some phony mediums around here. They used Ouija boards. What? Have you been talking with Sophie Mathews? You're delusional."

I returned the board and Sophie to the counter, and decided to tell Detective Presley Warren the truth. To his credit, attentively, without interrupting or calling me nuts, he listened. We sat silently for a while. He started tapping his finger against the tabletop. "I don't believe any of this."

"I don't care."

"What?"

"Whether or not you believe me is irrelevant. I'm not looking into all this for a story or for myself. I'm doing this for Sophie."

Sophie trembled, and Presley stared at the pointer chattering against the game board. I looked him in the eye. "She's crying. Who was Roy Compton?"

Roy Compton had been a casual friend of Sophie's eighteen-year-old brother. They were both on the high school football team. Compton won a football scholarship to the University of Ohio and left for school at the end of the summer of 1966.

"Was he a suspect in Sophie's murder?"

"Not according to the reports."

"Was he at least interviewed?"

"The only time his name is mentioned in the report is on a list of the brother's friends that was given to the police. There is a brief mention of the supposed whereabouts of the friends at the time of the murder. Most of them—including Roy Compton—had alibis."

"Who was his alibi?"

"A bunch of drunken friends and his mother."

"Airtight, huh?"

"You think this Compton guy killed Sophie?"

"Sophie told me Roy killed her. She couldn't remember his last name."

"She can't remember the name of the guy who murdered her? Seems to me that would be something a person would remember."

I ignored the sarcasm. "Do you know Brian Mathews' phone number?"

"Why don't you look him up in the phone book?" He raised that eyebrow.

"I already did. There are eight Brian Mathews listed in the phone book. I was just about to start cold-calling when you got here."

"Can't Sophie use some of her voodoo and give you his phone number?"

Sophie flew across the kitchen, whacked him upside the head, and clattered to the floor.

"*OW!*" he yelped. "*What the devil?*" Rubbing the side of his head, Presley glared down at the offending plastic pointer. "Let's pretend I believe all this and look into the whereabouts of these men. What do you plan on doing with the information?"

I picked up Sophie and set her gently on top of the game board. "I am going to find Roy Compton."

He shook his head as though to clear it and stood in preparation to leave. I called out a challenge before he got to the door: "Hey, Detective, whoever locates Brian Mathews first has to pay for dinner."

He grinned over his shoulder. "Deal."

Sophie and I played YES and NO for a while concerning her brother until she got tired. Then I had an epiphany. I searched the Web for obituaries for Sophie's parents. Her father, Ronald, died at the age of seventy-seven in 2008. Her mother, Margaret, died in 2011 at the age of eighty-one. I decided that the funeral home listed for Margaret would likely have a contact number for Brian. I would call the funeral home in the morning. If that wasn't successful, I would start coldcalling the eight people in the phone book.

The next morning I went to the funeral home and told the lady pretty much the truth. I bought something at a yard sale that had belonged to Brian's murdered sister, and I wanted to return it to him. She offered to call the number Brian had provided at the time of his mother's funeral and give him my name and number.

Back at home I set Sophie and her sack on the kitchen counter and crossed to the phone. The voice mail light was flashing. I retrieved the message, and a male voice identified himself as Brian Matthews and asked, would I please return the call. At the sound of her brother's voice, Sophie went ballistic inside the plastic sack.

"Careful. You'll fall again," I cautioned.

I called him back but still refused to identify the something I was trying to return.

We got to Brian's house at 3:00 P.M. With Sophie safely nestled inside her plastic grocery sack, I rang the doorbell.

Brian Matthews was tall and easily forty pounds overweight. He invited me in to sit in the front room. He said his wife was at their son's house with the grandchildren; they have four grandchildren, their son having one boy and one girl and their daughter having two girls. The plastic sack rustled. I pulled the Ouija board and pointer from the sack to cover the sound. "I bought this at the yard sale. I thought you might want it back. I know what happened to your sister."

I handed him the board but held the pointer in my hand. He turned over the board and frowned. "You bought this at our old house on Powder Run?"

"Yes. There was a piece of masking tape holding the pointer to the board. Your sister's name was on the tape," I lied.

"My mother told me she had forgotten a box of Sophie's things in the attic. She couldn't bring herself to retrieve them." He sighed and handed the board back to me. "Thank you for coming over, but you can keep the game. There isn't any memory of her in there for me."

I was struck by both the eloquence and the irony in the statement. He started to stand as though to cue my leaving, but I strove on. "Mr. Mathews, I need a little bit more of your time…if I may."

He settled back in his chair.

I gave him pretty much the same story I had given the funeral home lady. Plus, "I've been in contact with a Detective Presley Warren about your sister's case."

"My sister was murdered in 1966. The police followed every possible lead at the time. The local newspapers trotted out the story in 1976 and then again in 1986, but the case still went nowhere."

"Science has come a long way in the last twenty years. Detective Warren told me Sophie was wearing a heart-shaped ring with embedded diamond chips on the day she died. The police record shows the ring was returned to your parents. Do you have the ring, Brian?"

"Yes, I have it. Why? What does her ring have to do with anything?"

"Sophie likely fought with her attacker. His DNA could be on that ring."

I awkwardly pointed at my left ring finger while still cradling Sophie. "Little bitty gemstones can collect a lot of stuff. Has the ring been professionally cleaned?"

"No; that is, not that I am aware of. Assuming there is DNA, you need to have a suspect for comparison. The police exhausted the possibilities."

"I have been reviewing the police files and going through the interviews," I lied. "There was a friend of yours who was never interviewed by the police. Do you remember Roy Compton?" I held my breath.

"Sure, I remember Roy. He was on the football team."

"Brian, if Sophie fought her attacker and he was injured…possibly on the face…" I made a raking motion with my left ring finger. "After the murder, did anybody turn up with cuts on his face? Roy Compton maybe?"

He stared straight for a bit—raised his eyes toward the ceiling—and then let his eyes roam around the room, as though the memory lurked among the living-room furniture. I saw it in his eyes the moment he captured it. "Roy had stitches." His voice shook, and he pointed above his left eye. "Here."

"Was Sophie right-handed?"

"Yes…she was."

"So, if she struck out against her attacker, she would have connected with the left side of his face?"

Brian nodded and continued in a voice thick with emotion, "Roy said he stumbled over something in the garage. He had been drinking beer with a bunch of guys over at the high school field. He said his mother had to take him to the emergency room for stitches. Sophie was pretty. Roy looked at her. All the guys looked at her. She never told me he had bothered her or anything. Surely the police would have checked out his alibi?"

"He claimed he was drinking with friends, went home, fell, got stitches, etc. It would have been easy to fiddle with the time frame. The boys had all been drinking. Roy's mother probably believed what she wanted to believe."

Brian put his face in his hands and sobbed brokenly. "All these years—oh my God, Sophie."

I didn't want to leave him alone after what he had just remembered. He called his wife to come home. He told me Roy Compton played on the University of Ohio football team. He got picked up by the NFL and played two seasons with the Kansas City Chiefs as a linebacker. Brian said Roy was a mountain of a boy/man. He got injured somehow and ended up coaching at small colleges here and there. The last time Brian had spoken to any of his old friends about Roy, they said he was semiretired and coaching a high school team in Murfreesboro; he didn't know which high school.

After Mrs. Mathews had returned home, I told Brian I would call Detective Warren to make arrangements to have Sophie's ring picked up. I called the precinct from my car and left a message on Presley's voice mail: "I've spoken with Brian Mathews. He has Sophie's ring. He said he remembers that Roy was sporting stitches above his left eye the day after Sophie's murder. Roy Compton is supposed to be working as a coach at a high school in Murfreesboro. I don't know which one, but I'm going to find out. I'll call you when I know more. I told Brian you would arrange for Sophie's ring to be picked up for forensic testing. You owe me a dinner, Detective." I gave him Brian's phone number and disconnected. I reached into the well of the passenger seat to grab my laptop. Pushing back my seat to give myself room, I opened it and said, "Let's find Roy Compton." Sophie's sack rustled.

I found him on a website for Forest High School in Murfreesboro. It was now a little bit after 4:00 P.M. I was familiar with Murfreesboro. It would take us forty-five minutes to get to Forest High School.

I arrived at the school and was reaching for my tote bag when my cell phone rang. It was Presley.

"Where are you?" he barked.

"Sophie and I tracked Compton to Forest High School in Murfreesboro. We're at the school."

"I did the same thing. I'm halfway to Forest. Wait for me in the parking lot."

I noticed a man exiting the school from a side door. Without saying good-bye, I disconnected, climbed from the car, and hollered, "*YOO-HOO!*"

The man looked over. "Can I help you?"

I trotted toward him. "I had an appointment with Coach Compton and I'm late. Do you know if he's still here?"

"Yes, he's here." He pointed to a blue truck. "That's his." He held the door open and directed me to the gymnasium. "He's probably in his office back there. We are hosting a football day camp next week. You can go on in. I've locked the doors. You can get out, but you won't be able to get back in."

"Thank you," I said, and hurried into the school.

My sandals sounded like rifle shots clacking across the gymnasium floor. Pushing my way into the locker room, I heard noises coming from an open doorway. A large man abruptly stuck his head around the corner of the doorway. I jumped.

"Sorry if I startled you. I heard you coming."

I took a shaky breath. "Coach Compton?"

"Yes, ma'am. Are you here about the day camp?"

Roy Compton was indeed a mountain of a man. He had to be six-foot-four easily. He was solidly built for a sixty-five-year-old.

"Have a seat," he offered as he circled the desk.

"No thank you, Roy."

He paused and squinted across the desk. "Do I know you?"

"No, but you knew a good friend of mine a long time ago."

He smiled. "Is that right? Who was that?"

"Sophie Mathews." I answered flatly.

The smile dropped from his face, "I'm sorry...who?"

"You remember Sophie. You killed her forty-seven years ago. She was only fifteen. You're sure you don't remember?"

He shook his head. "Look, lady, I don't know who or what you are talking about."

I set the plastic sack on the desk. "Sophie was a pretty little thing."

He nodded enthusiastically. "Yeah, sure, I remember the girl who drowned. She was the sister of one of my football buddies. I didn't have anything to do with Sophie's death. I wasn't even at the party that day."

I continued, "You were obsessed with her. You knew she was going to be at the birthday party that day. You hated that she was with Jake Thorne. You got drunk and went to the park. You probably parked on the other side of that stand of trees by the lake. You planned to sneak up on the party and spy on Sophie. Instead, you saw Sophie and Jake by the willow. You watched them through the trees. You must have been furious with her."

He rounded the corner of the desk. I stepped back at his approach but kept talking. "After Jake left, you surprised her. You argued. Before she could scream, you grabbed her by the throat. She cut you with her ring, didn't she?" I pointed casually at his face. "I can see the scar where it dissected your eyebrow. She didn't die a passive death. She made you work for it. She marked you. Things have changed a lot since you killed Sophie. Take DNA, for example. I have the ring," I lied. "It hasn't been cleaned. I imagine all those nooks and crannies surrounding the diamond chips are loaded with your DNA."

He advanced. "No...no...I didn't."

"There was a witness, Roy." He stopped in midstep. "You wrapped your ham-sized hands around her neck, lifted her clear off the ground, and carried her stiff-armed into the lake. Sophie drowned, but only after you tried to wring her neck."

Roy stood slack jawed and stammered, "N-No one...was there."

"Sophie was there."

God engineered the human structure to accommodate only one soul. Sophie swept through me with tremendous and glorious rage. "*How dare you!*" we screamed. A gash appeared above Roy's left eye, and blood ran down his face. "*How dare you steal my life!*" Our voice twisted into an anguished wail. "*It was my life...mine.*"

Roy Compton stared in horror and crumpled heavily to the floor. Shielding his face, he sobbed through bloodied hands, "I'm sorry, Sophie. I'm so sorry."

Sophie maintained her splendid fury for a few seconds longer. I could feel her relief and reluctance as she let go of the rage that she had nurtured for forty-seven years.

Sophie withdrew the hair tie from my clumsy ponytail and dropped it to the floor. With sensual pleasure, she slowly raked fingers of both hands through the loosened strands. We inhaled and released a cleansing breath, savoring the corporeal sensation. Sophie was preparing to leave. I felt her soul swell with joy at her impending release. As I felt her leave, I was consumed with sadness over the loss of my young friend. Sophie wiped tears from our eyes.

"Thank you," she whispered across my mind. The essence that had been Sophie was gone. My vision blurred, and my heart ached with the forfeiture of my friend.

Roy lay in a sobbing, sprawling lump on the floor, blood no longer covering his hands.

I don't know whether Roy Compton will ever pay for his crime in the legal arena. His confession might be manipulated by the skills of a good attorney. Would there be traces of his DNA on Sophie's ring? I don't know. What I do know is that Sophie Mathews is free.

A loud crash, followed by thudding footsteps echoed across the gymnasium floor. "LIV, OLIVIA, SOPHIE?" Presley was coming for us.

My eyes found the plastic grocery sack sitting on the desk. Sophie was on a spiritual journey to a better somewhere. I sank to the floor and waited for Presley.

The Ouija board—The Mystifying Oracle—and the pointer thingy sat silently on the desk in a plastic sack, an inanimate parlor game.

LINDA S. BROWNING's short story *No Wake* won first place in the Mystery Times Ten 2013 writing competition. The cozy mystery featured Leslie and Belinda, two widowed heroines with overactive imaginations. They were such a hit with readers that they now star in their own series. Buddhapuss Ink released the first two books, *Daredevil* and *Shanghaied* in 2015. Linda rediscovered her love for creative writing after retiring from her day job as a social worker. She shares her home in Tennessee with her husband, a thirty-year-old Amazon parrot, and an eighteen-year-old finch. Linda invites you to join her at lindabrowning.net.

Third Place

Pesticides Can Kill You

Kim Kash

PESTICIDES CAN cause all kinds of health problems; in fact, they can kill you. This is what Phoebe Dayton explained to the customers and neighbors at the Greenview Organic Farmers Market. Phoebe was Greenview's market master, and she warned her neighbors and customers about pesticides frequently, and at great length. In fact, a few complaints had come in over the years about her fanaticism on the subject of organic farming, but most people shrugged it off. Heck, most people in Greenview agreed with her. Why wouldn't they?

The Greenview Organic Farmers Market was held every Saturday from May through early November in the city hall parking lot. Twenty vendors sold fresh fruits and vegetables, fresh baked bread, locally roasted coffee, free-range poultry and eggs, grass-fed beef, cheeses and butter, honey and beeswax candles, and locally made organic skin care products. Everything sold at the market was grown or produced within a hundred miles of Greenview, a suburb Washington, DC.

Every Saturday during the market season, Phoebe walked from her tiny house at the edge of the woods surrounding Greenview, arriving at the parking lot before 7:00 A.M. There she set about making sure everything was ready for the day's market. She walked the lot in her sensible Birkenstock sandals picking up stray scraps of trash and set up the market's information table, making sure the card file of seasonal recipes was organized and stocked. Phoebe's wide-brimmed straw hat, ringed with bright silk flowers, covered her short, reddish curls and protected her aging but well-maintained face from the morning sun.

The farm trucks began arriving shortly before eight: plain, white box trucks with farm names stenciled on the sides rumbled in along with dusty pickups and stake body trucks piled high with watermelons and boxes of tomatoes and yellow squash, eggplants and sunflowers, peppers and zucchini. Susan, who roasted coffee in a DC warehouse, chugged into the lot each week in an ancient brown Volvo that looked like a coffee bean on wheels. Cassie, who made goat cheese on her farm just north of Baltimore, usually arrived at about the same time.

Phoebe was there to greet each vendor with a cheery wave and a hello, and pitched in to help with setup whenever anyone was short-handed. All the farmers were well practiced in setting up for market: they could pull in, pop up their shade tents, set up their tables, and have their goods displayed and signs up in about an hour. The blacktop blossomed into a beautifully bright farmers market. Phoebe thought it looked like a patchwork quilt or flowers in a field.

Phoebe ran a tight ship. Vendors who were in violation of any market regulations—inadequate signage, displays extending into the public walkway, expired scale inspection stickers—were issued warnings promptly at the opening bell. By thirty minutes past opening, Phoebe issued fines. Fortunately, she didn't have to use these tactics very often; vendors would quickly fall in line after their first offense. Plus, the market was so successful that vendors just learned to accept Phoebe's ironclad rule enforcement as a price of doing business.

Frank McNeill was one of the newest market vendors. He and his wife, Sarah, ran a small farm near Easton on Maryland's Eastern Shore, not too far east of the Chesapeake Bay Bridge. The McNeill farm stuck to the Maryland basics: strawberries, summer squash, tomatoes, corn, watermelons. They weren't interested in heirloom varieties or the more obscure vegetables such as Brussels sprouts or mesclun salad mix.

Phoebe first visited the McNeill farm in March, shortly after they signed on. Frank had just tilled the fields and was getting seedlings started in a long greenhouse behind his aging white farmhouse. Several small, weathered barns and outbuildings were scattered around the fields near the house, and the rutted tracks in the land held water from a recent rain, reflecting an overcast sky. Frank and Phoebe took a tour through the fields in Frank's battered blue Chevy pickup truck, and he pointed out the different fields as they drove. "Spinach just went in over here. There on the left is where the squash and pumpkins'll go in. Past that we'll do the corn."

As they bumped across the muddy fields in the truck, Frank told Phoebe that the farm didn't have organic certification but that he had stopped using chemical fertilizers, herbicides, and pesticides. Phoebe explained to Frank that, while the Greenview Farmers Market is an organic market, they try to support farmers who are making the transition from "traditional" to organic farming methods. She laughed mirthlessly at how odd it was that "traditional" in this context meant "chemical dependent."

"How can we keep poisoning the land like that?" she fumed, animated as she always was on the subject of pesticides. She clutched the tote bag in her lap so tightly that her knuckles blanched white. "I shudder to think of all the chemicals that American children eat every day, and we just sit back and let it happen. Do you know," she exclaimed, turning her flushed face toward Frank, "that this generation of American children is expected to have a shorter life span than the previous one? Did you know that? And it's because of our diet. It's all that high-fructose corn syrup and chemicals these days. It's poison!" With shaking hands, she reached into her bag and pulled out a tissue and wiped a bit of spittle from her upper lip. She crushed an empty plastic soda bottle on the floor of the truck cab beneath her feet with a furious crunch.

Frank cleared his throat and turned the truck toward the farmhouse. They rode back in silence.

At the house, Sarah joined Frank and Phoebe around an old but sturdy gray-and-white Formica table in the kitchen. Sarah put out a glass plate of store-bought coffee cake and made a pot of instant coffee. Phoebe declined both with a prim shake of her curly red hair. "Thanks, but I try not to eat or drink anything with pesticide residue. You know how that goes." She laughed. Sarah recoiled, the smile dropping from her face. Frank looked away.

"So what was it that finally made you decide to switch to organic farming?" Phoebe asked Frank pleasantly, all trace of her earlier outburst gone.

"But—" Sarah started.

"Sarah, you let me talk about the farming," Frank interrupted. "My family has been working this land for three generations. Farming's all I know, and I guess you gotta do it different these days. Don't want to be poisoning children...."

Sarah shifted uncomfortably in her chair, and Frank's pale-blue eyes squinted as he peered out the window, across the fields. The ticking of the kitchen clock was startling in the silence.

Phoebe and Frank finished up the necessary paperwork that afternoon, and she congratulated him on being accepted into the select pool of Greenview Market vendors. Frank and Sarah saw Phoebe out shortly after that, standing on the porch and waving as she turned her Ford Escort around on the gravel apron and made her way down the long drive to the blacktop road.

Phoebe wondered about the tension between Frank and Sarah as she drove west, across the Chesapeake Bay Bridge and through the suburban sprawl around Washington. Was Sarah unhappy about Frank's new and possibly financially risky farming venture? Was Frank lying about his organic practices? She didn't see any evidence of pesticide use, but she also knew that there was no way she could tell just from one brief farm visit.

As she merged onto the Beltway and around to Greenview, she decided she would have to keep an eye on the McNeill Farm offerings. Not for the first time, Phoebe wished she could keep a closer eye on all her vendors. How could she know what they were doing out there on their farms while she was miles away in the suburbs? Could she trust them to grow their crops without poisons? What more could she do to protect her food supply, and that of her neighbors? She felt a heavy weight of responsibility on her shoulders. She took a deep, resolute breath and drove on.

When the market opened in early May, vendors arrived with berries, lettuces, and asparagus, spinach, and other cool-weather greens. Organic producers have an easier time at the beginning of the season if the weather cooperates because there are fewer pests when it's cool out. The McNeill offerings looked fresh and perfect, but so did that of most of the other vendors.

As the market progressed into summer, lettuces gave way to zuc-chini, berries finished up as peaches, and beans and corn ripened, and the tomatoes arrived. In July and August, Maryland farmers markets explode with tomatoes. Some farmers have signature items, such as squash blossoms, or sunflowers, tomatillos, or okra, or Japanese eggplant. But come high summer, every farmer brings tomatoes to the market. In late July the Greenview Market was bursting with Beefsteaks and Romas, beautifully striped and mottled heirloom varieties, yellow pear tomatoes, cherry and grape tomatoes. Shoppers would load up their bags, wagons, and SUVs with this summer delight. They would haul home tomatoes in anticipation of homemade spaghetti sauce and salsa, BLTs, Caprese salads, and simple plates of slices sprinkled with salt, pepper, and olive oil.

One searing-hot morning in August, almost every vendor had mountains of tomatoes to sell. Phoebe had been watching; she had been noticing Frank's produce all season, and it was finally the tomatoes that did it. Frank's tomatoes were just too perfect. His stand looked like the produce at the local Safeway: pretty but sterile. There were no scarred or split fruits, none with insect damage. Customers were flocking to Frank's squared-away stand though the tomatoes he had cut for sampling were not as fall-over delicious as the funny-looking heirlooms, in Phoebe's opinion. Regardless, McNeill Farm was doing a landslide business selling pretty tomatoes—so much so that Sarah came to the market with Frank to help with sales. The other vendors were squawking behind Frank's back that he must be buying his tomatoes from the wholesale market; Phoebe was suspicious.

"How do you grow such perfect tomatoes?" she asked Frank that day as he hauled yet another box of round, red fruits from the back of his truck. "None of them are split or scarred from insect damage. Are you using row covers? What's your secret?"

Sarah leveled a cool gaze in Phoebe's direction from where she stood behind the stand's cash register, then turned back to continue serving their long line of customers. Frank gave a little, lopsided grin and said, "Must be that nice, light Eastern Shore soil." The soil there does tend to be light and sandy, but Phoebe didn't believe that was all there was to it. The market's two other Eastern Shore vendors were having a terrible time with insects and fungus this wet summer.

Phoebe's eyes narrowed under her flowery straw hat, and she

glared at Frank. "I don't believe you. I think you're using pesticides."

"Well now, Phoebe—" Frank raised a placating hand.

"I will find out what you've done, and you will pay for it," she said in a low voice.

A chill ran through him and Frank stood speechless for a moment. Then he regained his composure, shifted his weight and barked out a laugh, turned his back on Phoebe, and carried the box of tomatoes to the front of his market display. He caught his wife's eye and looped his finger around his head in the universal "she's crazy" gesture, and the two of them turned cold gazes back to Phoebe. She pursed her lips, then turned on her heel and continued her market inspection rounds.

On that steamy Saturday, Phoebe knew she needed to take action. She had done it before; she would probably have to do it again. It wasn't her favorite part of the job, but Phoebe was dedicated and not one to complain when she had to roll up her sleeves and get to work.

At about 9 o'clock the next evening, Phoebe's Escort drove east across the bay bridge, past Kent Narrows, and into the flat, green Eastern Shore farmland. She listened to a tape of old *Prairie Home Companion* episodes as she drove, chuckling at the News from Lake Wobegon. She turned left just past Easton onto the rural, blacktop road that led to the McNeill farm. She pulled off to the side of the road just past their driveway, tucking the car into a grove of trees rather than leaving it exposed in the wide, flat landscape on this bright, full-moonlit night.

Phoebe pulled a camera, flashlight, and her rubber-coated work gloves out of her tote bag. She slipped out of her car, closing the door gently behind her. Crossing a weedy drainage ditch and squeezing in between two corn plants as high as the proverbial elephant's eye, Phoebe set off at a quick pace down the row toward the farm buildings. The night was slightly breezy, and the corn rustled gently in the moonlight. The farmhouse glowed white, every window dark.

As she reached the end of the row of corn, Phoebe came out onto the track that the farm trucks used to travel between fields. She remembered that this was the track that she and Frank had traveled down in his blue pickup in the spring.

Parked right at the end of the row of corn was a farm truck with a tow-behind trailer. A fifty-five-gallon drum was strapped on the trailer, its flat bottom positioned flush with the back of the trailer and attached to a sprayer mechanism. Forward of the drum, sitting just behind the trailer's hitch, was a small pump engine and several hoses that attached the engine to the drum and the sprayer. Phoebe had seen this kind of simple tow-behind sprayer at other farms; she knew that the engine powered the pump to spray the contents of the drum in a fan-shaped pattern behind it. The sprayer could be hooked up to a drum of just about anything, from organic fertilizer to Agent Orange. This particular drum was labeled diazinon.

Phoebe stopped in her tracks. Diazinon! An organophosphate insecticide, it had been banned from golf courses in the late eighties because it kills birds by the thousands—but it was still permitted for agricultural use. Phoebe's jaw clenched in anger. Organic-farming practices, eh? Phoebe had done a little nocturnal farm touring before, a bit of behind-the-scenes fact-checking, but never had she found such a flagrant example of chemical use on a farm claiming to use only organic methods.

Thinking that any damning evidence would likely be in one of the farm's outbuildings, Phoebe had been prepared to take photographic evidence of any wrongdoing and confront Frank McNeill with it. Standing out here in the open though, she didn't want to risk using the camera with its flash. So she shone her flashlight carefully into the open window of the truck cab and found several empty soda bottles on the passenger's seat. She reached in and grabbed one, then crept around to the pump engine, crouching behind the trailer hitch. With gloved hands, she carefully unscrewed one of the hoses near the engine and filled the soda bottle about a third of the way full with the brownish liquid.

That'll do, she thought. If he tried to deny using diazinon and gets rid of the barrel, Phoebe would have this little bottle as proof.

As she began to reattach the hose to the pump engine, a dog's bark cut through the quiet summer night. *The McNeills don't have a dog, do they?* Phoebe didn't think so, but she was rattled. She quickly turned and ran back down the row, and reached her car in less than five minutes. Carefully, she eased the Escort out from under the trees and onto the blacktop road. She turned on her headlights as she rounded the corner away from the McNeill farm.

Phoebe made the return trip to Greenview in just under two hours, blasting Garrison Keillor all the way home. She was wired and knew she would have to drive back to the Eastern Shore the next day to confront Frank with her evidence. She pulled into her tidy driveway and marched into her trim little house, the cat meowing its protest at her unseemly hours.

The next day, Phoebe was scheduled to make a late-morning presentation about healthy eating at the senior center. She dashed home afterward, ate a quick goat cheese, alfalfa sprout, and heirloom tomato sandwich, and was on the road east again by 1:00 P.M. She turned onto the gravel drive of the McNeill farm at about 3:30. The August sky was a sun-bleached blue, and the trees on the far side of the crop rows looked dusty and limp. The air was still, and when she stopped her car on the widened gravel parking area near the house, not a sound carried through the hot air. The place looked deserted, and she guessed that the day's field work was done, having started in the relative cool of early morning.

Phoebe turned off the car, put on her rubber-coated work gloves, and picked up the soda bottle of diazinon, which she had double-bagged in two paper grocery sacks and buckled into the front passenger seat. As she got out and slammed the door, she jumped at the sound. Her dirt-encrusted hiking boots crunched across the gravel parking area, and she could almost feel the heat of the sharp rocks on the bottoms of her feet.

She walked up to the old clapboard farmhouse, with its broad, shady front porch. Her boots were noisy on the steps, and she knocked firmly on the front door. Silence. The afternoon still was complete; it was too hot even for the birds to bother singing.

After a moment Phoebe walked back across the gravel parking area and into the first set of fields. The truck with the tow-behind sprayer was facing a row of corn, having made a right turn from the track dividing the fields. She walked toward it, wading through a sea of Beefsteak tomato plants, neatly staked to about shoulder height.

She emerged on the other side of the row onto the track and turned left. Then she saw him. Frank was sprawled on the ground next to the sprayer's pump engine, his legs collapsed under him like a dropped marionette. He was covered in brown fluid that was growing sticky as the hot sun dried it on his skin, hair, and clothes. Frank's chin and chest were splattered with chunks of vomit, coagulating and drying in the heat. As she drew closer, the smell of every kind of human excrement enveloped her.

Then she saw that the hose connecting the pump to the chemical barrel—the hose she had unhooked during the previous evening's reconnaissance—was disconnected and dripping brown liquid. Evidently, when he had turned on the sprayer pump, the hose had shot loose, and diazinon had splattered all over the engine and trailer, and all over Frank.

As Phoebe stared, his chest heaved weakly, and his whole body twitched and convulsed. His encrusted eyes opened and focused on her, and he reached weakly in her direction. Then they closed again, and his hand dropped to the ground. A moment later his labored breathing ceased.

"I told you that stuff was poison, Frank," Phoebe murmured.

She turned on her heel and walked back through the field of tomatoes, holding the paper bag of purloined diazinon gingerly with both hands in front of her like a big bag of dog poop, cleaned up after someone else's pet. (Phoebe had plenty of experience with *that*.) Back at her car, she opened the door to let some heat escape and had a careful look around.

Frank and Sarah's old Chevy pickup truck was nowhere to be seen. Sarah must be out. Phoebe got into the car, buckled her seat belt, put the car into reverse, and did a careful three-point turn. She went down the drive at a quick but careful speed and turned back onto the blacktop road. She sped away from McNeill Farm, never passing a single car.

As she drove through the commercial strip of Easton on Route 50, Phoebe pulled into a gas station. She paid cash to top off the Escort's tank, and, with a gloved hand, dropped the paper bag with the bottle of diazinon into the Dumpster behind the station. Then she got back on the highway and drove west, across the bridge and home again.

At the next market there was a gap in the row of produce vendors, and several of Frank's regular customers stopped by the information booth to ask after him. "I haven't heard from him," she said, sounding slightly annoyed. "Perhaps there's a backup on the bay bridge this morning." Everyone was looking for Frank's perfect tomatoes. Phoebe directed them instead to the farm stands belonging to Joe Reilly and Findlay Hill Farm for a lovely assortment of organic heirlooms and slicers.

She also made sure the stack of literature about the dangers of pesticides was displayed prominently on the market information table. She couldn't emphasize that enough.

Pesticides can kill you, you know.

KIM KASH is the author of two novels in the Jamie August series: *Ocean City Lowdown* (2013) and *Ocean City Cover-up* (2015), as well as the best-selling *Ocean City: A Guide to Maryland's Seaside Resort* (2009). One of her short stories will be included in *Chesapeake Crimes: Storm Warning!*, the seventh volume of the Chesapeake Crimes anthology, scheduled for publication in 2016. Kim lives in Maryland and the Middle East. Which can be weird. You can find her at KimKash.com.

Wheels of Fortune

Georgia Ruth

I KNOCKED, and eased the door open. The room appeared vacated, but I knew Aunt Rose was expecting me. Light from the hallway spread across the neatly made hospital bed and her travel clock and tissue box on the nightstand. On the pillow, a stuffed kitty cat waited for her return.

"Josie? I'm back here, honey." A wavering voice came from the shadow of the thick blackout curtains favored by insomniacs.

My sight adjusted, and I saw a figure in a wheelchair squeezed into a corner.

"Hi! What are you doing in the dark?"

"Resting my eyes." Aunt Rose placed arthritic hands on the large wheels to propel the chair forward. I turned on a lamp. As usual she was immaculate. Her curly hair subdued, she was wearing a blue shirtwaist dress, knee-high hose, and washable terrycloth slippers, a birthday gift from me. Today's tissue was tucked into her fabric belt. My aunt was dressed for a trip to the mall, but we would spend the day here at Sunset Home.

I bent to kiss her cheek, catching a whiff of the lavender soap she favored. "Our Thanksgiving feast isn't ready yet. Do you want to take a stroll outside?"

"That sounds delightful." She smiled, always the gracious hostess.

I hid my handbag in the armoire and took the navigator's position behind her wheelchair. We rolled down the carpeted hallway past the nurses' station, where several of the staff waved and commented about how pretty she looked. One young man had just returned to work after a motorcycle accident kept him hospitalized for several weeks. While he was convalescing, he often stopped by the nursing home to tease the staff.

"How's my favorite Southern belle?" Max limped over to hug Aunt Rose.

"I'm doing great. And you better not gobble up all our food. I've seen how you youngsters eat."

"There's plenty for everyone." The charge nurse pulled off her glasses, letting them dangle on a cord around her neck. "But I'm keeping an eye on this one."

We all laughed. I was grateful for the staff that chose to work that day. The charge nurse told me that she and several others tried to schedule themselves on holidays so employees with families could have the day off to celebrate with them. There was a genuine family feeling to this gathering, and I was happy to be part of it.

We took the elevator to the main lobby, where French doors exited into the landscaped courtyard protected by the four wings of the building. I eased the wheelchair down the slight ramp and walked the perimeter, admiring the jaunty colors of the potted nasturtiums and begonias surrounding a small fountain in front of a windmill palm tree. We waved at Clemmie, who was sitting at an umbrella table reading to her husband. She was dedicated to battling Alzheimer's with him. I stopped Aunt Rose's chair next to a bench under a pergola covered in bougainvillea and plopped down to rest my always aching feet.

My job behind the cosmetic counter at Macy's was becoming hazardous to my health. A promised fast track to management had not taken place, and I had the varicose veins to prove it. I wore chinos to hide my ugly support socks, but fretting was useless. The heat of the sun was relaxing, and I closed my eyes.

"Honey, did I tell you I'm getting married?"

"Really, Auntie? How nice." I was used to the mental lapses of an eighty-year-old. She must be thinking back in time to her marriage to Uncle John, gone for twenty years now. He had climbed to the top of the law enforcement ladder in Washington, DC. Aunt Rose had been a homemaker and relied on his pension.

"Abraham is so handsome," she said softly.

I jerked my attention toward her. "Abraham the orderly? The black attendant? What are you going on about?"

"Oh, he's so nice. And so strong. He can pick me up and put me in bed like I'm as light as a young girl."

"Aunt Rose, that's his job to help you. The ladies can't pick you up. And your legs are very weak." I'd been worrying about my legs, but Aunt Rose had worse trouble with hers. Fortunately, she had the resources to afford a private room in a comfortable nursing home. When I'm her age, I won't be able to afford a corner lamp post as a bag lady. I could see myself hunkered down on the pavement, useless legs beneath me.

"My mother used to say, if you don't use it, you lose it." Her blue eyes twinkled.

I rousted myself from my pity party. "Are you walking every day?"

"Maybe I could use my walker more than I do. Some days the staff doesn't have time to help me."

I was overwhelmed with guilt. Aunt Rose was my only relative from the last generation, and I neglected her. I vowed to do better.

Abraham came out to announce to everyone in the garden, "Happy Turkey Day. Dinner is served, ladies. And gent." He waved at Clemmie and her husband.

"Kind sir, will you do the honor of wheeling me in?" Aunt Rose fluttered her skimpy eyelashes in his direction. And added a huge grin when he agreed.

"My pleasure, Mrs. Cohen." Abraham looked at me and shrugged his broad shoulders. All in a day's work for him, I was sure.

Most of the residents had gone out with family on this Thanksgiving Day, so the main dining room could easily accommodate everyone. It looked like an elegant hotel restaurant with moiré wallpaper above the varnished chair rail and wainscoting. Assorted colorful prints were artistically grouped. The home was lovely, but I had been surprised when my aunt wanted to move in here. I thought she'd been doing great living alone.

I didn't know much about her before she moved to my seaside Florida village five years ago. She told me she was ready for year-round sunny days, the same thing said by most elderly newcomers. I had settled here a while back after my husband and son were killed in a car crash. I found peace walking the beaches. I thought perhaps Aunt Rose was acting as a surrogate mother, and I was grateful for the effort. She bought a condo near me and seemed to enjoy a busy social life, often visiting out-of-town friends for weeks at a time. We bonded while respecting each other's privacy. I drew strength from her wise counsel when I worked up the courage to ask advice. She inspired me to stand up for myself.

Abraham parked her in front of an empty place setting at the end of the dinner table, and I slipped into an upholstered chair beside her.

Her nemesis, Eva Bergen, was already seated at the head of another table. My aunt had told me about their conflicts over everything from hairdresser appointments to television shows in the lounge. An aide whose beauty was marred by runaway acne stood next to Mrs. Bergen, slicing turkey into bite-size pieces that she ate with her fingers.

"Abraham, please cut my turkey," Aunt Rose said loudly. She seemed to glow with pride at his assistance. But I could see that he was giving equal attention to the needs of the eight others at our table: precisely cutting, admonishing, teasing, and praising the efforts of the self-motivated.

Abraham pulled up a chair across from me. "Do you want a plate, Mrs. Lauter?"

"No thank you, Abraham. It's my day off, so I slept late and had a big breakfast, enjoying the calm before the Christmas shopping storm."

"Do you two already know each other?" Aunt Rose piped up cheerfully.

"Just here, Auntie. I don't think Abraham purchases much in women's cosmetics."

Abraham patted her shoulder, and I would have sworn she blushed.

A request from someone at the other end of the table demanded Abraham's attention. He unfolded his big frame and pushed back his chair. "Duty calls." He had to be good-natured to respond with a smile on his face to the needs of many. I didn't know if he chose to sit with us because I was a new voice or because he really was interested in my aunt. Some thoughts are best pushed to the back of the brain.

During the course of a wonderful dinner of turkey garnished with whole cranberry sauce, cornbread dressing, green beans, and sweet potato casserole, most of the residents dropped dinner exhibits on their clothing in spite of the huge holiday napkins spread on their laps or tucked into the neckline of those with shaky hands. Several no longer bothered with forks. Although many assured me the food was delicious, with all the lip smacking and slurping and assorted other noises, I had no appetite. What did that say about my personality?

We chatted with the others about the weather and historical events while Aunt Rose ate her dinner. I noticed a sweet-tempered attendant removing turkey and cranberries from Mrs. Bergen's clothing before wheeling her away. At the same time, Abraham was helping another woman leave the room on a walker. He held the end of a padded belt secured around Mrs. Frank's waist as she progressed slowly with chin held high. When Mrs. Bergen passed her, she shot out her hand and grabbed the walker hard enough to unsettle the unsuspecting senior. But Abraham was fast to stabilize his charge. She regained her balance and growled, "Bullies don't scare me, Eva."

The young woman pushing Mrs. Bergen's chair scolded her. "Mrs. B., that wasn't nice. You could have caused Mrs. Frank to fall."

"Would serve her right. That floozy is flirting with my boyfriend."

Abraham immediately said, "Miz B., honey, you know you're the only one for me. Be sweet now."

Mrs. Bergen got this idiotic look on her face and smirked, "Well, I'll see you later then."

Mrs. Frank snapped, "You're the floozy."

The aide and Abraham exchanged grins. Oh, the patience their jobs must require.

I wheeled Aunt Rose back to her room so she could rest. In the hallway we passed the rolling meds cart from which an RN dispensed prescriptions to those who were bedridden. May had a frown on her chubby face as she counted the pills poured out of one bottle. She looked up from her sheaf of paperwork and smiled at us. "Mrs. Cohen, did you have a nice Thanksgiving dinner? I'm so glad you invited your niece."

"Do you two know each other?" Aunt Rose looked at me with the clear-blue eyes of an angel.

"I've seen May when she comes into your room with your nighttime meds. They help you sleep, remember?" I said.

"I don't need them. I never took them at home. Only here, at May's.

By the way, dear, you have a beautiful place." She smiled at the nurse.

May squeezed her hand and kissed her cheek. "Thank you, Mrs. Cohen. I'm so glad you like it here."

Tears burned my eyes, and I gave the nurse a grateful nod. Aunt Rose had been institutionalized only four months but seemed to be failing fast. I felt as though I wasn't doing enough for her. I had tried only one time to take her away from the nursing home. We went to a restaurant because the doorways of my small apartment would not accommodate the wide wheels of her new chair. We were both of average height, and she was slender, but I had a difficult time trying to maneuver her by myself. I had investigated the prescriptions she was being given, but I couldn't argue with a doctor who was very cautious and wanted to keep her comfortable. And the nurses seemed very careful with the dosage. I didn't know what else to do.

We watched the television show *Wheel of Fortune* sitting in wingback chairs she had moved from her condo. If Aunt Rose wasn't sleeping at night, I didn't want her to lie down for a nap. A telephone call interrupted the program. Aunt Rose smiled when she answered. "Everything seems to be quiet for now. See you later." I was too well mannered to pry into her business, but I was curious.

The following show was a special about the troops celebrating the holiday away from home, and we both dozed off.

A nurse awakened us with a reminder about the musical event in the social room. I promised to stay a little longer and wheeled her down the hall to share the excitement. Rows of chairs formed a semicircle around a piano decorated with fall leaves and a cornucopia of plastic fruit next to an unlit candle. At the doorway, Mrs. Bergen pushed past us, whizzing in the opposite direction. Everyone got out of her way.

A thoughtful volunteer had given up her family plans to play the piano and sing show tunes for the shut-ins. She also brought her little dog, who woofed in time to the music and chased his tail for the finale. After the show the pint-size entertainer went to each person to receive a pat on the head and loving words. Most of the residents were delighted, but Aunt Rose was distracted. She kept looking over her shoulder. I worried that her nap would keep her from sleeping through the night.

When I wheeled her back to her room, she said, "It's strange that Eva wasn't in the audience." We peeked into Mrs. Bergen's room, but it was empty. It was a mystery to me why Aunt Rose wanted to find her enemy unless she was checking up on Abraham, too. We talked awhile, and she fidgeted. I finally excused myself late in the afternoon before supper was served.

On my drive home, I thought about the pills that May was counting. I had seen a similar pill in my aunt's trash can. But what did I know? I needed to assert myself more and ask questions. My mother's older sister had come when I needed help, and now I should be strong for her.

I left my shoes and purse in my bedroom and wandered to the kitchen for a snack. The message light on the answering machine was blinking. A nursing home representative had called to tell me there had been "an incident" but not to worry. What did that mean? Then I heard the *Titanic* theme song in the background and hurried to retrieve my cell phone, but I was too late. It was the nursing home again.

Whatever the incident, my aunt needed me. I hurried out the door and sped back to Sunset Home. Driving my aged Corolla like a maniac took most of my concentration, but I kept reciting the most critical portion of the message: "Mrs. Cohen is all right, just shaken up." As fast as my swollen feet could move in my geriatric sneakers, I skirted the police car and ambulance and rushed to the main entry. Some of the residents were returning with their families, and the authorities were trying to keep up with who was where, and when. A uniformed cop at the door had to confirm my identification and receive permission to allow me to enter. I saw yellow tape at the end of the hallway where the EMTs were working. A crime scene?

The nurses' stations were vacant, and I didn't see any residents. Hallways were busy with uniforms of all kinds: doctors, nurses, police, EMTs, cafeteria workers, attendants. Close to me, one of the staff opened a patient's door and called out, "Are you okay? We're going to leave the door closed for a little while. There's a snake loose, and we're trying to catch it."

A snake? I trotted down the hall. I saw Mrs. Frank's grandson idling outside her room and spoke to him as I passed. "What's going on?"

"My grandmother was murdered." His eyes filled with tears.

I halted. "How? Who? Why?"

"By Colonel Mustard with a lead pipe in the library for all I know," he grumbled. "I got a phone call with shock and condolences. Shoot, she had already been taken to the funeral home. Very quietly, so as not to disturb the patients who might think there's an epidemic and try to flee. I can't get one intelligent answer to my questions, and I'm hanging out here until I do." He raked his fingers through dark hair. "I told my folks this place had too many accidents, but they liked the location."

"I'll let you know if I hear anything. I'd better see about my aunt. I think she was hurt."

"I saw the paramedics coming out of her room with an empty stretcher, so hopefully she's okay." He slumped against the wall with arms across his chest.

Envisioning the worst scenario for dismissing EMTs, and imagining it was too late for their help, I hurried to my aunt's room. She lay on her back on top of her bedspread, hands folded over her waist. I approached her quietly. Only a lamp on her nightstand kept the dark away. I saw her chest rise and fall, and took a deep breath myself.

Her eyes flung open. "Hi, honey. I suppose you heard the news?"

"About the snake?"

"No, that's some crazy cover story." Her forehead crinkled. "I'm talking about the murder. Mrs. Frank was killed two doors down! My heart hasn't beat this fast since my wedding night." She swung her legs over the side and sat up. Aunt Rose appeared to be unhurt, almost energized.

"Do they know who did it?"

"If they do, they're not telling me." Her eyes shone brightly. "Why don't you go out and investigate? Come back as soon as you learn something." She reached under her pillow and removed a pill that she threw in the trash can by her bed. "I never swallow these things. I try to sleep during the day when people aren't sneaking around in the halls."

I was confused. She seemed to wander between confidence and dependence. "Have you buzzed the nurses' station to complain?"

"Some people roam because they can't sleep, like me. But once in a while I've awakened to see somebody in here spying on me."

"That's creepy. I didn't know you were afraid in your room. I'll speak to the director."

"No, no. There was nothing to report until now." Aunt Rose sighed. "I didn't expect her to hurt Mrs. Frank."

"Her who?"

She cast an uncomfortable glance in my direction. "I shouldn't have said anything. Go on now. Find out what's happening."

I opened the door, and looked up and down the hallway. At the end was an anxious crowd surrounding a nurse's aide they'd backed against a wall. I got there late, just in time to hear the poor girl swear on her mother's grave that she knew nothing about what had happened. She was allowed to escape, and I had to get the story from the person next to me. It was Clemmie, who was here at all hours. Her brown eyes were rimmed in red, the only sign of her inner turmoil. Her blond coiffure was always perfect.

"What have you heard?" I asked her.

"Mrs. Frank was hit on the head while she was in her bathroom, and nobody saw anyone suspicious. Except for Mrs. Bergen, who reported seeing a strange man, wearing a hat and a trench coat, coming out of the room."

"Trench coat?"

"Yeah. Nobody paid her much attention. She's delusional."

"Does Mrs. Bergen ever have any visitors?"

"Her people are hours away. I think she admitted herself to a nursing home so they can't find her. But maybe they haven't tried too hard." She looked over my shoulder. "Hey, Marty."

A tall man in a golf shirt and black slacks smiled and came toward us.

"Hey, Clemmie. I hope Winston is having a good day. We miss him down at the precinct. I want to talk to Mrs. Lauter here." He turned his long, dark eyelashes toward me. "I understand from the nurses that there seems to be a continual altercation between your aunt and one of the other ladies."

This guy had a smooth voice, like chocolate syrup. I was attracted, but I was loyal to my aunt. "Aunt Rose? She's too old to altercate with anyone."

"Age doesn't change personalities. The witness who saw a man leave Mrs. Frank's room thinks he may have gone into Mrs. Cohen's room. Did she say anything about it?"

"No, she's as curious as everyone else."

"Can I talk to her? With you present? I don't want to disturb y'all."

I thought this guy could disturb me anytime. "Yes, I'll introduce you."

We walked down the corridor to my aunt's room. She was leaning back against the pillows with a book in her hand. She looked wary when we entered, and I apologized for not warning her.

"This detective wants to ask you a few questions."

"About the murder?"

The detective was quick. "Yes ma'am. My name's Detective Foley. Why do you think there was a murder, Mrs. Cohen?"

"The halls have been buzzing with clusters of residents, staff, and uniformed strangers. I'm feeble, not deaf."

Aunt Rose's feisty demeanor showed a marked contrast from earlier in the day. She seemed like her old self. I really needed to ask questions about those morning meds.

"Did you see anything that might help us?"

"I saw Eva Bergen wheeling rapidly down the hallway shortly before an aide entered Mrs. Frank's room and screamed."

"Was your door open?" the detective asked.

"I opened it to peek out because I heard the whirring noise of a wheelchair when everything should be quiet. I knew somebody was roaming."

I interrupted. "How did you get into your chair by yourself?"

Aunt Rose raised one eyebrow at me. "People have to adapt to survive."

What did that mean? Now I was really suspicious about Abraham and how much adapting was involved. Was he romancing my aunt?

"Was Mrs. Bergen alone?" Detective Foley asked.

"Yes. There was no one else in the hallway."

"Were you alone?" I asked her.

"Of course."

A knock on the door preceded the entrance of a gray-haired man wearing a suit. I was glad to see Aunt Rose's doctor.

Detective Foley looked confused. "Saul Stein, what's the FBI doing here?"

"We're working undercover, and I'd appreciate your discretion."

"Of course." Detective Foley looked from him to me to Rose. "Sorry."

I wasn't undercover with anyone. Was my aunt?

Amid more commotion in the hall, an aide entered with a supper tray. Detective Foley sighed. He said he would be in touch if needed and handed his card to me with his personal cell number. I clutched it. My head throbbed, and my heart stuttered.

The man who I thought was Aunt Rose's doctor asked her if she was hurt. When she told him she was fine, he left the room. She refused to answer my questions and calmly picked at her food. What in heaven's name was going on?

I stayed with Aunt Rose until she requested a nurse to help her get ready for bed. I could tell she was exhausted. I didn't think I could sleep when there was an evil force still stalking the helpless elderly. Her tale of a watcher in her bedroom frightened me, especially since Mrs. Frank's grandson mentioned accidents. Was he afraid to say fatalities?

I made arrangements to camp out on the sofa on a balcony over-looking the lobby. The lights were dim except around the nurses' stations, where two professionals were on call on each of three floors.

A shrill alarm woke me. I went from a deep sleep to standing up ready for flight. The night nurses were running down a corridor, and I followed. At the end of the hallway near a window, two figures in wheelchairs rammed into each other like gladiators. As I trotted closer, I saw my aunt and Mrs. Bergen pulling hair and scratching each other. Mrs. Bergen threw a fist toward my aunt's face. She ducked. A nurse and I pulled the chairs apart, and somebody shut off the fire alarm. My nerves quit screaming. Aides from the other floors were responding. One pulled out a cell phone and said she would call security.

"Wait a minute, Ruthie. Let's ask some questions before the answers are forgotten." The charge nurse turned to Rose. "Can you tell us what happened, Mrs. Cohen?"

"She snuck into my room, but I wasn't asleep, and I shoved her into my bathroom and jumped into my getaway chair. It's faster than walking." She paused to take a breath. "I was almost out the door when Eva caught me and forced me away from help at the nurses' station. I pulled the fire alarm because she tried to clobber me with a candlestick."

"Okay, Ruthie. Call the police."

"I should get a chance to tell my side of the story," said Mrs. Bergen.

"Go ahead."

"I was minding my own business, going down the hall, when this crazy woman rammed into me."

"You know that's not true, Eva," said Rose. "You have no shame."

"What about the candlestick lying on the floor back there?" The charge nurse glowered at Mrs. Bergen.

"Never saw it before."

"There were two on the piano before the singing," said Ruthie. "But one was missing afterward. Housekeeping is looking for it."

"See, anyone could have grabbed it. It wasn't me." Mrs. Bergen whined, "You're all against me."

"We'll get the police to find out whose fingerprints are on it," said Ruthie.

I stepped over to hold my aunt's hand. "Your face has some red welts, Auntie. Do they hurt?"

"A little. But not like a dent in my head like Mrs. Frank has." She pulled out her tissue and wiped her eyes.

"How did you know that?" I was startled by her quick response. I leaned over Aunt Rose in the brilliantly lit hallway. Several dark dots contrasted with her superfine white hair. "You have red in your hair, too. Those look like tiny cranberry seeds. There's another one on your shoulder. How odd."

The charge nurse put on her glasses to investigate.

The closest nurse to Mrs. Bergen picked up her hand and turned it over. I saw that cranberry sauce from our Thanksgiving dinner was still lodged under her long red fingernails.

"Maybe this is how Mrs. Frank got cranberry in her hair," said Ruthie. At my look of surprise, she said, "Detective Foley told us to keep that detail to ourselves."

The charge nurse muttered, "Congratulations, you kept a secret for five hours."

Mrs. Bergen raised her chin defiantly. "I have never let anyone take my man away from me, and I'm not going to start now. Abraham is mine!" She glared at Rose. "And for your information, I've eliminated better competition than you'll ever be." Before she could be stopped, she spun her chair and wheeled as fast as she could toward the elevator.

Three nurses raced after her, surrounded her, and pushed her chair into an empty room. The police arrived ten minutes later, and they took charge of the investigation. On-call nursing home personnel came in to calm the residents who had been awakened. Detective Foley arrived, and I heated up.

"We never know who rolls among us," said May, giving me a comforting hug. She misunderstood my flushed cheeks.

I rolled Aunt Rose back to her room. The FBI came again, and this time Saul explained to me that Rose had worked for them for years. Because of her "seniority," her current assignment was investigating the high number of *accidental* female deaths at Sunset Home.

"I'm afraid I'm not the agent I used to be, my dear." Rose looked sad.

"Well, you had me fooled, if that's any consolation. You put on quite a charade."

"We learned there was still an old warrant out on Eva Bergen from years ago under a different name. Her husband's death was suspicious, but her advanced years probably helped her elude capture. When Saul asked for my help, I agreed to take part in one last caper. But I wasn't up to the task."

"Excuse me, I saw you in action. You seemed pretty tough to me." I patted her hand. "I look forward to hearing your stories, if they're not confidential."

"My career is ancient history now. A stash of prescription meds was found in Eva's room along with property belonging to other patients. We think there might be evidence that some of those accidental deaths were overdoses. When she confronted Mrs. Frank, Eva was armed with the stolen candlestick and a wicked temper."

"Rose has been invaluable to our agency," said Saul. "She can share lots of stories with you since most of it is public knowledge, anyway."

"Since I'm older than dirt?" It was good to hear my aunt laugh.

After her FBI friend left, Rose yawned and got ready for bed. She abandoned her façade of weak granny in the wheelchair. As she snuggled down under the covers, she told me she was grateful for my watchful presence, but it wasn't necessary. She felt confident she would be moving back to her condo the next day. I was thankful she was as sturdy as a pillar of rock.

May's orders had not yet changed, and she came in with a sleeping pill that Rose pretended to take. Before I left, I stole the tablet out of the trash can so I could be rested to face Black Friday's chaos in the morning. I planned to borrow my aunt's fortitude to request a transfer to a different department. I wanted her to be proud of me.

I look at wrinkled faces differently now. Individuals with a long past and a short future have a story. Most of them deserve respect, but Abraham assured me, "A mean heart doesn't soften with age." He ought to know. I still wonder about him when I am out with my detective friend.

Ⓐ Ⓤ Ⓣ Ⓗ Ⓞ Ⓡ

GEORGIA RUTH lives in the foothills of North Carolina and writes a historical blog about her neighbors who have deep roots in the area: georgiaruthwrites.us. A member of Short Mystery Fiction Society, she has short stories published online for *Stupefying Stories* and *Bethlehem Writers Roundtable*, and in print in *Mystery Times Ten 2013*, *That Mysterious Woman*, and *History & Mystery, Oh My*. Her latest story, "The Mountain Top," came out in June in the Sisters in Crime anthology *Fish or Cut Bait*.

Stranger at the Door

Kate Fellowes

FATHER DEXTER crouched down in the deserted choir loft. The boys had left ten minutes earlier, and one of them had forgotten his math book. While tidying up, the priest had spotted it, pushed beneath a pew.

The church was quiet, now that the sounds of young voices and stomping feet had faded away. Had he ever been that young, he wondered, not for the first time. At forty-five, he was still in the prime of life, doing the work he'd been chosen to do, and yet he could feel his enthusiasm being replaced by sheer fatigue.

But that couldn't happen this week. This week, Our Lady of the Holy Family was playing host to a traveling exhibit of religious artifacts on loan from the Vatican. As art treasures went, these weren't much: a cross of semiprecious stones, an antique chalice, and a bejeweled ring said to have once belonged to Pope Sixtus. Still, standing beneath the church's leaking roof while admiring the glint and spark of the gemstones, Father Dexter was struck by a certain irony. The church had taken out additional insurance for this week—money they could little afford—to protect these three pieces. Wouldn't that money be better spent another way? Perhaps, a way that would put warm food in empty bellies or caps and gloves on cold, homeless citizens?

But enough of that, he told himself. Such questioning would lead nowhere. Next week, the artifacts would move on, and the parish could get back to real work.

It was while he was crouched down, arm stretched straight out to retrieve the textbook, that he heard a noise where there should be none. Up near the sacristy there had been a thump and a creak. The door, heavy and in need of oiling, made those sounds, he knew. But who could be there? And, more frightening, why?

The priest leaped up, book forgotten. The treasures were there, in the closest thing the church had to a safe: an old cabinet with locking drawers. Heart thumping, blood jumping in his veins, he moved quickly to the railing of the loft as another thump signaled the closing of the door.

What he saw stunned him into frozen silence. Coming down the aisle of the church in no apparent hurry was a priest. A black hat pulled low over his eyes hid the man's face, but the white of his collar was easy to spot. In his crossed arms he carried the cross, the chalice, and, Father Dexter presumed, the ring.

"Hello, there! Wait!" Father Dexter shouted, waving his arms. "What are you doing?"

The other priest glanced up just long enough to catch Father Dexter's eye and then took off at a clip, running with his arms pressed tightly against his chest. His footsteps rang heavily on the tile floor, but Father Dexter didn't hear them as he rushed for the stairs.

This couldn't be happening! What on earth was going on?

"Oh no. Oh no. Oh no," he chanted, praying he would be in time to intercept the thief.

When he reached the bottom of the staircase, the man was six feet in front of him, in the church vestibule.

"Stop! Thief!" Father Dexter used his booming voice.

His only reward came when the other man spun around, the chalice in one hand. Aiming quickly, he hurled it at the priest.

Closing his eyes and ducking his head, Father Dexter received a glancing blow on the shoulder, followed quickly by another.

The clatter of precious metal hitting old, cracked tiles forced his eyes open. Around his feet, the chalice wobbled on its side. The cross had skidded into the food drive barrel against the wall. When he looked up, the door to the outside was quietly easing shut.

Father Dexter rushed onto the porch, his head swiveling to catch sight of the thief. The church was on a steep hill. If the man had gone to the right, he'd be over the top of the hill by now. To the left there was an unobstructed view of shop fronts, restaurants, and taverns. In the dim light of evening, he couldn't be sure, but it looked as if a dark figure had just entered the tavern on the corner.

He made a quick decision. He picked up speed as he headed downhill, pounding the pavement. Momentum carried him a few feet past his destination as he stumbled to a stop and yanked on the tavern's door.

Jukebox music blared out, spilling into the evening. Soft light from within illuminated a room full of people, laughing and chattering.

All the men were dressed as priests.

Father Dexter stepped inside; his mouth was gaping. No one turned as he entered. He drew no attention at all. Just another priest in a bar, surrounded by women wearing too much makeup and not enough clothing. Nearly all wore red. Scarlet women. Father Dexter's brain processed the scene quickly.

Vicars. And tarts. It was the Vicars and Tarts party he'd seen advertised by the English-style pub.

"Oh no!" he muttered, sagging back against the doorjamb.

The thief could be any of these men. He would have had ample time to whip off his hat and blend into the crowd.

Eyes sweeping the gathering, Father Dexter looked for any indication of guilt or flight. A hasty exit to the men's room. A flushed cheek. A breathless puffing. But there was none. Still, he took the time to ask a few people if they'd seen anyone else enter a moment earlier. The answers brought no surprise. The revelers had seen nothing.

The father trudged slowly back up the hill, thinking gloomy thoughts. Only two objects had struck him in the vestibule, and a ring, no matter how big, wouldn't make much of a weapon.

"Oh please, let that ring be here too," he said aloud as he entered the church.

Kneeling to retrieve the chalice and cross, he held them under the light, looking for any damage. A jeweler would be necessary to check for loose stones, but there didn't seem to be any dents or scratches.

"Amazing! Amazing!" The father sent up a quick prayer.

For the next ten minutes he said other prayers, as well, but they went unanswered. The ring—once owned by Pope Sixtus—was nowhere to be found. With sinking spirits, he phoned the police and spent the next hour answering the questions of the two officers who responded.

"We'll do our best," Officer Pulaski assured him, but the policeman's expression wasn't very optimistic.

Father Dexter sighed. "Thanks, I appreciate your efforts."

"You know, you could have been injured, chasing a criminal. That was very foolhardy."

The priest pushed a shaky hand through his salt-and-pepper hair. "I realize that now. But, at the time—" he broke off, shaking his head.

"You say everyone knew about this exhibit, hm?"

"Yes, the whole community. There was an article about it in the *Express* just this week." An excellent article too, with a good picture of him holding the artifacts and smiling.

He wasn't smiling now.

The officers tipped their heads and exchanged a glance. One of them clucked his tongue. They may as well have said it out loud. Hopeless. Not a chance. Not a snowball's chance in— Well, he got the gist.

After the police had gone, Father Dexter spent a quiet hour trying to decide how to relate this disaster to the archdiocese. For fifteen years he'd been at this parish. His record was exemplary, clean and above reproach. The last thing he wanted was a blot on his copybook, but here it was, spreading fast.

It was after midnight when he tumbled into bed. His sleep was troubled, punctuated by nightmares. The bedclothes tangled around his limbs as he thrashed, once more chasing a thief down the streets.

The next morning when the priest returned from a very tense meeting with the higher-ups, the light on his answering machine was blinking. Automatically, he pushed the red button, listening to the voice that spilled out.

"This is the food pantry. We can't come by to pick up the barrel today. Our truck's broken down." A pause, a sigh. "Again."

Nothing new there. But it was too bad. The barrel was full, a testament to the generosity of the parish. Father Dexter forgot the news almost as soon as he heard it, his mind on bigger problems.

Later in the day, however, he had cause to remember it when a young man in overalls appeared at the rectory door.

"Afternoon, Father." He touched his cap. "I'm here to pick up the barrel for the pantry." The man spoke quickly, his hands shoved deep in his pockets. He didn't look the least bit familiar, which was odd. Father Dexter knew everyone.

"You must be new." He stalled for time while his brain did some quick maneuvering.

The pantry truck followed a regular pattern of breakdown and repair, but never had it been back in operation so quickly.

"Yeah. Just started this week," the young man replied, rocking back on his heels. He wasn't actually fidgeting, but he did seem a bit anxious. His eyes wouldn't meet the older man's, but then, that was awfully common these days.

Father Dexter opened the door a little wider, craning his neck to see the street. Parked at the curb out front was a truck with a rental company logo on the side. The back doors were opened wide.

Well, the group must have decided to do the pickups anyway, although renting trucks struck him as extravagant. Perhaps its use had been donated.

Jangling his keys, Father Dexter led the young man slowly around the building. He bit his lower lip as he thought.

If the pantry were resuming its schedule, they would have called to tell him. Why hadn't this young man mentioned the broken-down vehicle? And why was there a new person in the first place?

The key turned stiffly in the lock on the main doors, and Father Dexter had to use his shoulder to push them open. It was damp today, not quite raining, and the wood was swollen. In the dark vestibule, he snapped on a light, pointing out the barrel against the far wall.

"Thanks." The young man stepped around the priest. Gripping the heavy barrel, he tilted it up on one side, ready to roll it out to the street.

"You're going to have quite a time getting that into the truck without a dolly—especially at such an angle," Father Dexter commented.

The steep rise of the hill slanted the bed of the rental truck. If the barrel got away from the man, it would roll straight down, scattering cans of string beans and sauerkraut all over the block. Usually the driver pulled to the very top of the hill, where the road leveled off substantially, even though that point was nearly half a block away.

Muscles in the younger man's arms strained with the effort of moving the awkward bin, and little beads of sweat were apparent on his brow.

Watching in silence, Father Dexter pondered the situation. Surely everything was all right, just unusual. There was no need for the suspicion he felt. That had to be a result of last night's disaster making him doubtful and anxious. But what if his unsettled feeling was legitimate? What then?

"So, where's the old truck?" he asked, standing in the doorway, nonchalantly blocking the path.

"Um, doing the other side of the city." The answer came quickly and without elaboration. But it provided just the right information.

Don't confront a thief, the police had told him, and now here he was, facing one. This man was lying, coming to retrieve the one item he hadn't hurled at Father Dexter the night before.

The priest closed his eyes, recalling the scene. It would have been so simple to toss the ring into the barrel, planning to retrieve it later. He had never thought to look for it there, expecting it to be on the floor with the other treasures.

His heart thumped heavily, rapidly, and he felt his hands grow cold. How could he stop the man? What could he do, short of barring the door?

The younger man looked up at him. "Excuse me."

Father Dexter stepped aside. It would take the thief a good five minutes to load the barrel. Plenty of time for him to make a phone call.

The barrel scraped against the sidewalk.

"You know, I believe there are a few things in my kitchen for the barrel. I'll run and get them." The fib slipped out easily, and the priest took off at a dignified trot, around the side of the building and into the rectory.

His shaking hand closed over the phone as he punched in 911.

"This is Father Dexter," he whispered, eyes on the kitchen doorway. "The thief is here! Right now! Out front! Hurry!" He hung up, swallowing hard.

There. The deed was done. In no time the authorities would be here, and the crime would be solved.

If he was right.

Oh, these self-doubts were awful and unavoidable. If he was wrong, he'd look like a fool, and the ring would still be missing. But he'd had to act quickly. There was no time for second-guessing.

One hand still on the receiver, he stood, silently, listening to the sounds of the barrel being loaded onto the truck. A grunt. A thump. A muttered curse. The young man was still at it.

Father Dexter consulted the phone book and dialed once more.

"Paul's Rental World."

"Hello, Paul. This is Father Dexter. Say, did you rent a truck this morning? To a young man, about five ten, with dark hair?"

His parishioner thought a moment, then spoke. "Yep. About an hour ago. To Timmy Ward. Can't imagine what he wants it for, but I'll bet it's no good."

"Ward? Related to Dick Ward?" The town troublemaker was a constant challenge. Father Dexter had yet to bring the man into the fold.

"Yep. His cousin. Just back from a trip upstate." Prison, he meant. "Anyway, he took the truck, but just for the morning. I haven't been letting it go lately, but it's all I had today."

Father Dexter blinked, his throat tightening. "Why don't you rent it out?"

"Well, the engine's fine, but I've had a little trouble with the parking brake. Darn thing lets loose."

A chill spread up the priest's arms, raising the hair on the back of his neck.

"I told that kid about it though," the other man continued. "So long as he doesn't park it on a hill, it'll be fine."

The receiver swung back and forth from its own weight, dangling where it had been dropped. Father Dexter, fleet of foot, was out the door within seconds, his husky voice filling the air.

"Tim! No! Wait!"

But, of course, he hadn't.

The barrel was balanced precariously on the truck's back bumper, Tim struggling to slide it over the edge and into the vehicle.

Father Dexter was in time to see the look of surprise on the young man's face as the brake let loose. Tim gave a shout. The truck rolled slowly backward, and he staggered, his eyes darting swiftly around him.

"Get away! Get away!" The priest waved his arms frantically.

A few people on the sidewalk stopped to stare, at first not

comprehending. They remained frozen in horror as the tableau played out.

Father Dexter raced around to the front of the truck. If he could reach the controls, he could stop it. If he could open the door of the moving vehicle and climb inside…

His hand was on the door latch, his feet still in motion when the truck gave a ponderous lurch. The priest pressed his eyes shut, trying to block out the animal-like howl of pain that rent the air. Tim, trapped.

The barrel crashed, sounding like heavy thunder. A cacophony followed as cans rained onto the concrete. There was shouting. Then screaming. And behind it all, the wail of the injured man.

The truck door gave a metallic creak as Father Dexter at last jerked it open.

As he leaped inside, grabbing the steering wheel with both hands and pulling himself in, he could hear the blare of a siren. His foot found the brake, jammed it home as the shriek of the police car drew nearer.

In the rearview mirror, he watched the scene. A knot of people at the curb circling around the still form of Tim Ward. Red and blue lights speeding up the hill. Cans tumbling down, into the path of the oncoming squad car.

He bent his head, lips moving in silence.

Much later, Father Dexter walked slowly down the block, trailing a plastic garbage bag that he filled with the dented runaway cans.

Tim Ward had been taken to the hospital in serious condition after being knocked down by the truck and crushed under the falling barrel. Outside his door, the police were waiting to have a little chat when he regained consciousness.

Father Dexter bent, feeling drained. He lifted a container of baked beans from where it had been lodged against a sewer cover.

Beneath it, glimmering in the weak sunshine, lay the ring that had once belonged to Pope Sixtus. The priest paused. It was such a little thing to have caused such suffering.

Picking it up, he slipped it carefully onto his finger. Yes, yes. It would be safe there.

AUTHOR

KATE FELLOWES is the author of five romantic mysteries, most recently *Thunder in the Night*, which was a launch title for F&W Media's Crimson Romance imprint. Her mystery and romantic short stories have appeared in many publications, from Woman's World to Crimestalker Casebook. Working in a public library means every day is a busman's holiday for her. She blogs about life at katefellowes. wordpress.com/

A Prescription for Murder

Selaine Henriksen

MOM WAS really mad. She'd grounded me for two weeks because of the whole "could have been hurt" thing. She wanted to ground Gran too but, hah, as if. And she still wouldn't let me get a dog, not even one as cute as the one in the painting I'd found. She told me it was a papillon, which is French for "butterfly." Because of the dog's ears, I guess.

I still went to Gran's after school until Mom could pick me up. She'd be even madder if she knew I was hunting through that attic for anything else Gramps might have stashed up there. Gran was getting real tired of me hauling paintings down every five minutes asking if it could be a copy of one by a famous artist.

"That's one of your mom's," she said.

"Nope, one of your mom's."

"Your mom's."

"That's a poster. For heaven's sake, April May." My name's April, but she calls me April May for short, even though it's longer.

Turned out it was a poster from my mom's old room. Two horses nuzzled each other under an enormous tree in a green, green pasture. I liked it, and Gran said I could take it home. I unrolled it for Mom when she came to pick me up.

"I remember that. Nice to see it again." She glanced at it in passing, then took Gran's arm and led her into the kitchen. "Wait in the car, April," she called over her shoulder.

It took me a minute to roll up the poster again. Mom and Gran had their heads together, whispering. I crept a little closer. I was hoping they were figuring out how to surprise me with a puppy, but all I heard was my mom say "doctor's appointment." Gran snapped, a little loud, "Again?" Mom shushed her, and they glanced my way. I made like I hadn't heard anything and headed to the car.

I like to read detective books, all kinds, and I like to watch detective shows with Gran. I intend to be a detective when I grow up, or maybe a writer of detective stories. I'm not sure yet. My radar was pinging. Mom was seeing the doctor a lot. She didn't look bad, or sick. She had lost weight lately though. I worried it was cancer.

My thinking was confirmed when she took me shopping with her over the weekend and bought a bunch of new clothes. Even an itty-bitty bikini that showed off all the weight she'd lost. I was sure she was getting ready for a last hurrah before dying. Checking off her bucket list or something. Mom would get all tetchy if I asked her outright and tell me something about keeping my nose out of adult business, so I asked Gran.

We were sitting at Gran's kitchen table like always after school. She had her tea, and I had my milk and cookies. But I didn't feel much like eating. Worrying about my mom made my stomach churn.

"You're not eating, April. Something you want to get off your chest?"

I couldn't hold it back. "Is Mom dying?" I burst out.

Gran looked surprised. Then she laughed. "Well now, that came out of left field," she said. She stopped laughing when she saw the look on my face. "No, April May. What on earth would put that idea in your head?"

I told her about the weight loss, the pills she was taking, seeing the doctor every week, buying new clothes—and a bikini even.

Gran interrupted, laughing again. "She's trying to lose weight. Nothing wrong with looking your best."

"For what?" I demanded.

"For who, you mean." Gran winked at me.

"Who, then?"

Gran just shrugged. "Eat your cookies, dear."

It was true; my appetite was back after learning Mom wasn't dying. Of course, now I had another mystery. Who was Mom getting all pretty for? I ate a cookie and set my mind to working.

Mom was an art restorer, working at the university. Every time I'd been over there, all her colleagues were at least a hundred years old. With gray beards and stuffy accents. Except for Linda. She was the only other woman in the department. She was Mom's age, I think, and Mom's boss too, I believe. Mom was a professor, and Linda was a director. Linda and Mom were friends. Linda didn't have any kids, but Mom and her went out a lot together. You have to keep an open mind if you want to be a detective or a writer, so I knew it was possible Linda and my mom were an item. But it didn't make sense. They'd been friends for years, so I couldn't see that changing into dating now.

The next Wednesday Mom was trying on her new clothes. I was at the kitchen table slurping my cereal.

"What do you think of this?" she asked, pirouetting in front of me.

The shirt totally showed off her boobs. I frowned. "Are you going on a date?"

She sighed and tromped upstairs. She was back in a few minutes. Different shirt, looser.

"That looks nice," I said. "Who are you dressing up for?"

"No one. There's no harm in trying to look nice," she said. She washed down a couple of pills with her coffee.

"It's Wednesday. Do you have another doctor's appointment today?"

Her cheeks turned red. "Yes, I'll be picking you up a little late."

"It's him." My eyes got wide. "You're dressing up for your doctor? Isn't that kinda weird?"

"It's not like that." Her cheeks stayed red though. "I mean, no! Linda's seeing him too, you know." She frowned at me. "It's none of your business, April. And don't slurp."

See? Mom's always telling me stuff is none of my business. So I asked Gran.

Gran gave me a long look over her teacup. "Is this about your father, April?"

Talk about out of left field (whatever that means). My mom always said, "Your father is dead," and she always said it in the tone of voice where I couldn't tell if she meant *dead* or *dead to me*. I'd never met him. This was so not about him. To my mind, Gramps was my dad. I told Gran that, and she pulled me to her hefty bosom and hugged me tight.

"Besides," I said, "what do you mean about him?"

Gran brushed away a tear. "Well, I mean, maybe you think your mom shouldn't see anyone else because of your dad."

My birthday was in a couple of months. I was turning ten; I knew things. I think Gran meant like on TV where the kids contrive to get their parents back together. Like maybe I was holding out hope for that.

I nodded. "Because Dad's a spy. And we never see him because he has to stay away to protect us from the bad guys who would use us against him."

Gran's eyes got huge. She took my hand and patted it, staring into my eyes trying to figure out if I was on the level. I let her stew a bit.

I laughed. "Joking, Gran! I got you good."

"Oh thank God." Gran swatted at my head.

There was nothing funny about it when Linda died. Mom was in shock; that's what Gran told me to explain why Mom had gone from looking good thin to too skinny with her eyes bugging out a bit. Gran and I didn't go to the funeral because we didn't know Linda, really. Mom came back looking bad.

I held her hand as she blotted her eyes, and Gran made her a cup of tea. I couldn't think of anything to say, and I guess Gran couldn't either. Mom cried. Then there was a knock on the front door.

Gran doesn't use the living room much. She likes to keep it pristine. She lives in the kitchen, and we always use the back door. So I deduced it couldn't be anyone we knew. I was right. Gran led a police officer into the kitchen. I did recognize him, however. He was one of the officers who had arrested the art forger who had tried to take Gran's painting.

He remembered us too. He shook Gran's hand and mine. "Keeping out of trouble, I hope?" he said. Mom blotted her eyes again.

"How can we help you, Officer?" Gran didn't look friendly.

"Detective Brown." He cleared his throat. "I, uh, need to ask you some questions, Ms. Wilkerson?" He looked at Mom.

Gran scowled. "Well, do you or don't you?"

Detective Brown looked even more flustered. I wondered how professional he could be. I thought you were supposed to keep a poker face when you're a cop.

"Please, have a seat," Mom said. "How can I help you?"

He stood, shuffling from foot to foot. "I'd prefer we talk down at the station," he said.

Gran went into full-on mama bear mode. "Look here; she just came from her best friend's funeral." She got up into his face. "There's no way you're asking my girl anything without me around, buster."

"I am sorry for your loss," he said to Mom. "We just have to cross all the *t*'s and dot the *i*'s. You know how it is."

I nodded. "Indeed."

They all looked at me.

"Go on upstairs, April," Mom said.

There was no arguing, so I skipped out and thumped up the stairs. By the time I crept back down, Detective Brown had taken a seat. Mom's purse was open, with her stuff scattered on the table. Detective Brown held up two pill bottles and looked at them carefully. I couldn't hear too well because I was hiding behind Gran's big reading chair. I sure didn't want her to catch me, not in the mood she was in.

"...sa-same doctor. They're for thyroid problems, heart," Mom was stuttering. "Women of a certain age, he said." Then she was crying again.

I felt like rushing in there and chasing that Detective Brown out, but Gran was ahead of me. We're a team, Gran and me; we think alike.

"What motive could she possibly have?" Gran practically growled.

Detective Brown stood. "The only motive we can find is that Ms. Wilkerson here is next in line for Ms. Baker's job as director of the department. Money is always a motive. I'm sorry, Ms. Wilkerson, but I do need to ask you to come down to the station."

Mom packed up her purse. I slunk lower down behind the chair and watched as he led my mom out by the arm. Gran stood by the front door until the sound of his car was gone.

"You can come out now, April May," she said finally. Can't pull nothing over on my gran.

She went into the kitchen and worked her old rotary phone, calling a lawyer. Just like on TV.

"Are they going to arrest Mom?" I demanded.

"Over my dead body," Gran snapped.

"Mine too," I said.

"Listen up, April May; you are doing nothing about this. Got it?"

"But we're a team, Gran!"

"No. No team. My job is to protect you and your mom. Your job is to go to school and to not worry. You hear me?" Gran looked real stern, so I couldn't even talk to her about what I was thinking.

I stayed at Gran's that night. I didn't sleep too well, thinking about my mom in jail. The next morning Gran told me she'd made arrangements for me to go to my friend Pam's house after school. A gentleman from her aquafit class was taking her out to dinner, she said. Well, honestly. First Mom, now Gran. It didn't sit right with me that she was going out to dinner while Mom rotted in jail. I didn't say anything because I saw an opportunity, and I took it.

For my last birthday before Gramps died he gave me a whole detective kit. It was more like a spy kit, but he told me it was the same thing. You're trying to gather information or clues, to solve a puzzle, and it could be either figuring out what someone is planning to do or what they've already done. My mom was all "Don't encourage her, Dad." I remember him muttering back, "But it's what she likes."

I'd left it up in Gran's attic. While Gran was in the shower, I snuck up and found the kit in a drawer of an old desk. There was a microlistener that clipped to my ear for hearing faraway sounds. A pen with invisible ink that had micro-sized notepaper that hid in the handle and a decoder light. To be honest, none of it worked. I'd discovered that when I couldn't hear squat from the attic. It was all pretty useless. Except for the binoculars. They weren't toys.

I threw it all into my backpack anyway and ran out in time to make the school bus. Gran, in her bathrobe, ran after me with my lunch, reminding me sternly to go to Pam's after school. I smiled and nodded.

I had a bad day at school. Mr. Grant kept telling me to focus. Having Mom jailed for murder focused me all right. Just not on math. I didn't care that I was in trouble with my teacher. I was figuring to get into bigger trouble, anyway. I had no idea just how *much* bigger.

I did go to Pam's after school; I just didn't stay there. I told them there was a change of plans, and my mom was home early after all. Then I went to Mom's doctor and waited. Of course.

There were lots of women, all around my mom's age. Some were heavy, some thin, some thin with buggy eyes. They all came out of the doctor's office with little smiles on their faces and made appointments with the receptionist. My mom wasn't the only one who blushed over him.

"Can I help you, dear?" the receptionist asked, interrupting my thinking.

"I'm just waiting for my mom," I told her. Gran doesn't care for liars, so I always try to be at least a little truthful.

"And she is?"

"Right here," I said cheerfully, and followed a random woman out.

So then I had to wait in the parking lot. I used my deductive skills to try and figure out which car might be his. I went with the shiny black SUV parked off to the side. The license plate read DRSLIM. That was a clue.

Finally, he came out. He was handsome, I guess. Lots of curly black hair, and he was tall. The SUV *whoop-whoop*ed as he keyed the lock. He was still halfway across the lot. From my hiding place behind some nice shrubbery, I tossed my decoder pen behind him. When he turned to look, I climbed into the SUV and gently closed the door behind me. Then I dove into the second back seat. I was sure he hadn't seen me.

I was sure he hadn't seen me 'cause I was peeking between the seats and saw him take a gold ring from his suit pocket and slide it onto his finger. He was married and hiding it. I slid down low when he started the SUV and checked his rearview mirror. He drove a while. When he stopped and got out, he slammed his door hard. Then the rear hatch opened, and he leaned over the seat to look at me.

"Out," he ordered.

Well, I could hardly pretend I was there by accident, so I got out. It wasn't hard to force some tears; he didn't look friendly.

"I lost my mom," I cried.

He frowned at me. "In the backseat of my car?"

Before I could come up with something, the front door of the biggest house I'd ever seen flew open. A lady stood there, very thin, with buggy eyes that looked like her head was being squeezed.

"Oh, Davey, I'm so glad you're home! There's someone in the

house!" One hand clutched her chest. I gathered she was his wife. To be honest, I'd have put her as his mom. Maybe an older sister, to be nice about it.

Dr. Daveyslim looked at me suspiciously. He grabbed my arm, not gently, and pulled me inside.

"I'm sure it's nothing," he said to her all soothingly. "Did you take your meds today?"

She nodded. "My heart's just pounding," she gasped. "I called the police. They're on their way."

"It's just your imagination. You know how you are." He pulled out his phone. He patted her shoulder while he told the cops not to respond; his wife was just having an episode.

"No, Davey. There's someone here. In your office!" She took his arm and looked at him. "I'm not imagining things." She was practically begging. "Don't you hear that?"

He brushed her hand off his arm. We were standing in a ginormous hallway, bigger than Gran's whole house. The stairs curved up to the next level. We could all hear footsteps from a room up above, footsteps that would stop, then start again. Clearly someone creeping around up there.

"I don't hear anything," Dr. Davey said. "You should take your pills."

"I already did. I told you."

He sighed. "Take them again. For me, please."

The penny dropped, as Gran liked to say. "I wouldn't do that," I told Mrs. Dr. Davey.

She noticed me for the first time. "Who are you?"

"April May," I said.

"What?" The poor woman was so confused, and I was willing to bet it was the result of those pills.

"I hear footsteps too," I assured her.

Dr. Davey scowled at me. "Sit." He jerked me over to a bench by the door and sat me down, hard. A little desk stood beside the bench, and he pulled out a gun from the drawer. Not a big gun, but still.

I wouldn't have thought it possible, but Mrs. Dr. Davey's eyes bugged out even more. "I'll call the police."

"No," he said. "I can still make this work." He looked kinda excited, as if things were coming together for him.

He flicked the gun toward the stairs. "Go on, both of you."

"Davey, what is this?"

"I think he's trying to kill you," I told her as we climbed the stairs. "The pills aren't working fast enough, so he'll have the intruder shoot you probably." I talked real loud so whoever was up there would hear us coming.

Dr. Davey poked the gun in my back. "Smart girl," he hissed. "Now be quiet or you'll be the first to go."

I won't pretend I wasn't scared. You can't talk your way around a bullet.

We reached the top of the staircase. A long hallway with wood floors and dark-wood panels led away into the distance. The footsteps had stopped, and all was quiet except for Mrs. Dr. Davey's ragged breathing. She was crying but didn't seem all that surprised.

Dr. Davey pushed open the first door on the right and shoved me and the missus in ahead of him.

It was dark in there. Heavy curtains covered the windows, and glass bookshelves lined the walls. I took Mrs. Dr. Davey's hand and ran toward the large desk in the middle of the room. I crouched behind it and pulled her down with me. I noticed right away there was no chair there, which doesn't make sense for a desk.

That's because the desk chair came crashing down from behind the door onto the bad doctor's arm. He shouted and dropped the gun. Gran stepped out of the shadows and belted him with the chair again. He fell, reaching for the gun, but I scampered out and kicked it away from him. Gran sat on him. He grunted.

"Use your device, April, and call 911," said Gran. She meant my phone. I was happy to see her. We really were a team.

The woman on the other end of the phone sounded mad. "We already had a call from this address," she snarked, "then it was canceled. You can get in big trouble, young lady, for wasting police time."

"Call Detective Brown, please," I shouted. "Tell him it's April May and Gran."

Gran is heavy, but Dr. Davey was strong, and it looked like he was going to throw her off. Mrs. Dr. Davey scuttled out from behind the desk and grabbed the gun. She pointed it first at Gran, then me, then her husband.

"What's going on here?" she demanded. "Get off him," she yelled at Gran.

Dr. Davey stood and spread his arms, grinning wide. "Honey, these people are crazy. Give me the gun. The police are on their way." He scowled at me, then ducked as Gran swung the chair at his head.

He danced out of reach, toward the gun. Mrs. Davey put the desk between her and him, the gun shaking in her hand.

"Just give me the gun and everything will be all right," he said.

The two of them faced off over the desk. Gran had hold of me right quick and all but tossed me out of the room. My gran is strong.

"Run, April," she ordered. "Out of the house."

"What about you?"

"I'm coming."

She was huffing and puffing behind me as I booked it down the hallway. Footsteps pounded after us. We made it to the bottom of the staircase when a heavy hand fell on my shoulder and spun me around. Dr. Davey had hold of Gran too. She tried to wallop him again, but he was too quick for her. His eyes looked wild; things were getting out of hand. I don't know what he was going to do next because the front door banged open, echoing in the hallway.

Detective Brown strode in, looking very coppish and impressive. Especially when he looked up the stairs and pulled out his gun. I turned around, and Mrs. Dr. Davey was coming down the stairs holding Dr. Davey's gun. She sure looked like the crazy lady from someone's attic: rail thin, frizzy hair, eyes bulging.

"Put down the gun," Detective Brown ordered.

"Shoot her!" Dr. Davey yelled. "She's crazy."

The gun trembled in Mrs. Dr. Davey's hand. She was staring at her husband when a very un-crazy look crossed her face. She raised the gun at him.

"Drop it!" Detective Brown said, keeping his gun leveled at her.

I jumped in front of her. "No, it's him," I shouted.

Gran jumped in front of me. "She's right," she said. "Arrest this man for the murder of Linda Baker. And the attempted murder of his wife."

Dr. Davey made a break for it, but Detective Brown didn't hesitate. He tripped him and handcuffed him. Gran held out her hand for Mrs. Dr. Davey's gun. She held on to it, still pointing it at her husband.

"You'll never prove anything," she whispered. "He always tells everyone I'm crazy."

"Oh, I found the proof," Gran said. "He'll rot behind bars for a good long time."

Detective Brown stepped over and took the gun. He looked at Gran and me. "Why am I not surprised to find you two here?" He sighed.

Mom met us at the station. She clutched me tight and didn't let go while Gran laid it all out for Detective Brown. Dr. Davey was trying to kill his wife using a mix of medications for low thyroid function and high blood pressure. Not uncommon problems in *women of a certain age*, she said. I took that to mean my mom's age. She had discovered evidence that he had been experimenting on his patients to get the doses right for murder. And his motive? That huge house belonged to Mrs. Dr. Davey.

I had been reconsidering my career choices and thinking about maybe becoming a DRSLIM myself. So my mom wouldn't have to say all the time that everything I wanted was too expensive and so Gran wouldn't have to count her pennies. Detective Brown was right; money was always a motive.

"Gran," I whispered. "Did you lie to me? You were supposed to be at dinner."

"I did go to dinner," she answered. "I just didn't stay very long. You were supposed to be at Pam's." She frowned.

"I was. I just didn't stay very long." Before Gran could lose her temper, I added, "What were you doing in the house with the missus in there?"

"I thought it was empty. I called and *halloo*ed, but I guess she was in another wing."

Mom dropped her head into her hands. "I feel so stupid," she said.

Detective Brown reached out awkwardly to pat her back and then stopped, shuffled his feet, and coughed. I had an idea he kinda liked her, and that explained why he didn't seem so professional.

"Sometimes we don't see what's right under our nose," Gran said. She rolled her eyes at Mom, then tossed me a wink.

I grinned. I was glad we were a team again, Gran and me.

SELAINE HENRIKSEN has supported her writing habit by working many different jobs over the years, from bookstore clerk to research technologist. Currently a fitness instructor and mom to two editors-in-training, she lives in Ottawa, Ontario, where she is a member of Capital Crime Writers. She blogs at miss-selaine-ious.jesande.com/, reflecting an eclectic taste in reading, as well as writing, although she is a firm believer that at the heart of every good story is a mystery. Selaine's books can be found at: smashwords.com/profile/view/Bainer and amazon.com/Selaine-Henriksen.

Requiem for a Hit Man

Elaine Menge

FINDING CURBSIDE parking in the hospital district was always tough. For Jack—pushing sixty, hands like dead weights on the wheel—the hard part was squeezing into a spot once he found one, especially since he wore lenses so thick that anyone meeting him face-to-face would swear they were looking into the huge, round eyes of an enraged barn owl.

After many tries working the faded-blue VW's clutch with his sciatica-plagued left leg, shoving the stick forward, then plunging it down and back into a bucking reverse; he sandwiched the Bug between a Toyota 4Runner and an even bigger egg yolk-yellow Hummer. Patient, if unskilled, Jack didn't mind grinding it out while others honked.

He patted a gray towel on the passenger seat. Beneath the terry cloth nestled a Ruger Mark II in a shoulder holster, the leather cracking in spots after nearly thirty years of use. As if reassured by a friendly landmark, Jack smiled at the gray lump, then gave the spot to the left of his heart a pat.

His smile faded. Something seemed off. He wasn't sure what.

Next thing he knew, he was standing—wedged between the front bumper and the SUV—and peering into the Bug's little trunk.

He blinked hard. If he'd bothered to make this detour, it must have been for a reason.

Staring back at him from inside were stacks of *Women's Day* magazines, his mother's walker, a sack of dirty laundry, and a black violin case.

Only the violin struck him as having any importance. He grabbed the handle and lifted it out.

Jack ambled down the sidewalk, careful not to trip on uneven spots where tree roots bullied the concrete. "Step on a crack, break your mother's back." The rhyme sang in his head. Couldn't do that now, not that he'd want to.

He would have to toss the walker and magazines. The laundry was his. He'd been hauling it to his mom's on the day she died, over a month ago. Cancer.

Seven years earlier—an even more painful loss since she was only fifty-four—his older sister died too.

He'd never asked which kind they had, the same or different. Cancer did it. That's all he needed to know.

Sneaky, cancer ate you up a little at a time. If he could do anything, he'd shoot cancer to hell. Stomp it, burn it, torture it. Make it yell for mercy.

When he reached the corner, he waited for the walk sign. Jack obeyed traffic laws, driving or on foot. Otherwise, what did you have? People doing whatever they felt like. Chaos. Just like cancer, those diseased cells elbowing out the healthy ones.

Vans and trucks and SUVs roared past. Hardly any plain old cars. Everybody is riding high and fast, talking on cell phones, looking stressed.

Where's the fire?

As far as Jack was concerned, none of the people shooting by were doing anything all that important.

He was.

Important as a surgeon. That's how his agent, Phil, put it. Unlike a surgeon, Jack might perform only five operations a year, but those were enough to keep a roof over his head and pay his mom's bills.

Waiting at this particular corner though, he felt uneasy. The hand holding the handle of the violin case was damp, gripping too hard.

He shifted the case to his left hand. With his right, he patted the spot just to the left of his heart again.

The gun wasn't there.

He looked down, saw that he was carrying his violin. No Ruger under his arm, but here was the violin. What the hell?

He played in the city's Civic Symphony, an amateur, musically challenged group that gave free concerts. Jack sat with the second violins, second to last. The guy who sat last had a pinkie missing on his left hand, and the group had a policy of not turning anyone away.

Jack, lucky enough to own both little fingers, was just good enough to beat out the guy who didn't. He was pretty bad, but he loved music and knew when to hang back and pretend-play.

But why was he toting his violin now? The rehearsal wasn't until that night.

He backtracked, squeezed between bumpers again, and put the violin in the trunk. Peeling off his sports coat, he ducked into the driver's seat and looped the holster over his head, snugging it against his chest. He crabbed his way back into the jacket and exited the car.

Jack strolled down the sidewalk in the opposite direction this time.

At a crosswalk marked with broad yellow stripes, he stopped. Nothing looked familiar though he felt he'd stood at this same intersection many times in his life. Back then, it hadn't been marked with these stripes.

It hit him. His pediatrician had occupied an office in the medical arts building across the street from him. The building's stylized bird figures, pressed into the concrete above the doors and windows, jolted his memory.

Yeah. Dr. Swinnel.

After each shot Jack was awarded a sucker. They called them boosters. What exactly did they boost?

Swinnel was a young doctor. Jack recalled his thin sideburns, immaculate hands and pearly pink nails, his steely eyes.

Jack sensed Dr. Swinnel liked sticking in the needle more than handing out suckers.

His mother took him to McCrory's afterward. He'd circle the table that held the store's cheaper toys, knowing he could choose one, only one. "Getting just one makes it special," his mom said.

He found that was true.

From her he learned that his dad was a bad guy. He hurt people. Hurt his mom, and his sister.

Jack never met his father but always associated him with Dr. Swinnel.

The light changed. He wondered how many times it had done that since he'd been standing there, or since he'd first visited Swinnel. He looked back at his car, then forward.

The address?

He'd never needed one, always knew where he was going. Phil had booked the same room only two years ago.

There would be a girl—a new one, like the last one. She'd be the lure.

Then Jack'd show up. Two muted plugs into the guy would come next. *Thwop, thwop.* He checked. Yes, the silencer was in his jacket pocket.

The girl wouldn't scream. She'd scram. Jack would wait five seconds longer, make sure the guy was dead.

"The place I'm sending you, it's like an operating room," Phil had told him that first hit, way back. "You're a surgeon, cutting out gangrene, cancer, that multiplying shit. You're perfect for the part. Who'd guess?"

Phil, Jack's agent—he said to call him that—would now and then shove Jack's glasses back up onto his nose for him, firmly, with one finger. "What're these things?" he'd say. "Never seen glasses this thick in my life."

"Can't see without 'em," Jack admitted.

"And still you're a good shot."

"Oh yeah. A marksman."

"Amazing." Phil often used that word. "Amazing. You. A good shot. Lots of stuff in this life—there's no explaining. Just amazing, I say."

These days Phil drove a late-model Lexus. Jack cared nothing for luxury though his fees were important. Phil wore flashy clothes, jewelry. "The male peacock is the most glorious animal," he'd say. "Gotta look good if you want to attack the gals. I mean, attract." When he laughed at his own jokes, the last expiring chuckles stretched on forever.

"You should dump your day job," Phil would advise. "You're the best-paid moonlighter I know."

Jack guessed that was true and felt he deserved every penny of his fee. But now that his mom had died, the money didn't matter as much.

"You okay?"

The voice was musical. Jack turned. A young woman, twentyish, smiled. Fluffy bangs grazed her brows. She asked, "Need any help?"

Jack guessed he must have been swaying there on the corner for some time. He said, "Just got turned around. That's all."

He sensed a pullback on her part, if a well-disguised one. He knew his magnified eyes put her off. The lenses made them huge, scared looking, or angry. He wasn't either. He was just himself.

"You're sure?" She had a caring face, gentle, wide-set brown eyes. "I could call a policeman or somebody, to help."

"Just got turned around." He patted the spot under his arm. "Daydreaming is all." He crossed the street, the woman beside him. She tossed a smile over her shoulder and skipped ahead.

On the opposite corner, he watched her. Did his heart good to know there were still caring people in the world, even among the younger set. Now if only she could have told him where he was going.

Phil always wore a fat gold watch on his wrist and an even fatter gold pendant around his neck. Cancer the Crab—his astrological sign. "Not pretty sounding," he admitted, "but I like crabs, the way they skittle sideways. Crafty. You gotta be sly."

He'd summon Jack poolside, usually to the Peacock Inn, less often to the Hummingbird Casino. "I like hotels with bird names," Phil would say. "They're always dives. Nobody pays attention, and I'm the best-dressed guy there." He'd offer drinks and snacks, which Jack always turned down, then he'd tell him about the latest operation he needed done.

Today was the first time he'd hosted Jack *after* a job, one that never came off.

"What happened, if you don't mind my obscene curiosity?" Lounging in red trunks, hairy chest, the naked crown of his head daring the sun, Phil crossed his ankles and squinted so hard you'd think something thick and disgusting should ooze out of his tear ducts. "You're my go-to guy. Never let me down before."

"Yeah, you're right." Jack was hardly aware of resting his body against the lounger's bouncy slats. His body felt absent, especially his head. It might float off into the dusky heavens for all he knew.

A chubby kid belly-busted the pool, sprinkling both of them with chlorine.

"So, you want to explain why this Langston creep's still breathing?" Phil looked like fire might blister his lips.

Jack sat straighter and pressed his cuffs on both sides between thumbs and forefingers. "Just...circumstances. You might say they were different than usual."

"Different how?"

"I had to make some trips back to my car. Then my window of opportunity—that window was shut, ya know."

Phil's lips stretched into a big, rubbery smile. "Humor me. Tell me about these trips, back to the car."

It was an October morning, the first warm day after an early cold snap. Jack appreciated the sun on his shoulders—shoulders he always held tight and alert, like a boot camp private.

"The trips back to the car," Phil repeated.

"Right. The first one—I parked the car."

"Yeah?"

"Then I get out."

"Yeah?"

Jack shut his eyes. He remembered looking up and down the street. For what? A meter maid? No. He was looking with this feeling of not knowing why he'd come there in the first place. Then he'd pulled the violin out of the trunk. No use mentioning that to Phil.

"Yeah?"

"I start walking, to where you said. Almost got there. Then I realized. Forgot the gun."

"Forgot the gun." Phil tilted his head to one side. He sounded like one of those TV interviewers who repeat your last words with condescending disbelief.

"So I went back to the car. Got the gun."

"Shows promise."

"Then I started walking again."

"Walking. And then?"

"I got turned around. I guess."

"You guess?"

"Right."

"You went right?"

"No, I mean, yeah."

"And you walked to the apartment building? The whatsitsname? We paid Veda big bucks to set him up, don't ya know? Now we gotta do it all over, and Veda wants more dough."

"I didn't get to—that building—exactly. That's all."

"That's all?"

"Sorry."

"What's going on, Jack? You never screw up. Ice cream truck come by? You detour through some barroom, get kidnapped by space aliens? Catch Alzheimer's or something? You're my go-to guy."

Jack shook his head, abashed, but a lightbulb went off at Phil's last suggestion. Alzheimer's. Yeah. He'd heard about that forgetting disease. That's what it was. Must be. Shit.

"You can make this up to us," Phil was saying. "Next week. Same time, same place. This is getting time sensitive. Langston's due to testify. We need him gone—yesterday. Veda's sick of the creep. Let me remind you; the guy's a real piece of crap. Hurts people. Women."

Jack's eyes grew behind the thick lenses. "I don't like guys who hurt women."

"He does. Kids too."

"Shouldn't be breathing."

Phil arched his back. The water drops the belly-buster had splashed quivered on the thick hairs circling his navel. "I like you, Jack. Always have. You have standards. Won't kill a guy unless he's bad. Won't kill a woman, even if she is."

"Except that once." Jack clamped his lips together.

"Fooled you on that one. It'll be on my headstone, not yours."

"Wasn't even a bad woman."

"What woman ain't bad? Look, her old man needed a new life, understand? Kids are doing great, by the way. She was, uh, alcoholic, did drugs and all. Anything you can think of, she did. Believe me, Jack. Let that one go."

"She wasn't a druggie. No alkie either."

"Yeah, yeah, but getting back to Langston, he's a badass. Beats his kids, the wife. Lots of stuff I got on Langston. And you let him see another day, to hurt more people, not to mention he crossed Gemelli on that business deal, then squealed."

"Only when they cross Gemelli. That's when you call me. I'm getting it. Only when they cross Gemelli."

"Why not? They're still creeps. These guys come to my attention. I pass the facts on to you. The service you perform, society don't even know. You're one of those unsung heroes. Never win the Nobel Peace

Prize, but you get paid pretty good, right? I'm paying you good to rid us of Langston, but he's still kicking. Poor Veda. Poor girl, having to go through this all over again."

"I'll get him." Jack bowed his head. "Won't let you down."

He left Phil poolside, not sure where he was going next. This Alzheimer's thing, wasn't he too young for that? Didn't you have to be at least seventy?

The second try was scheduled for the following week. Same place, same girl.

Jack did better. He made it to the Cabana Apartments, with his gun, and without the violin. He rapped on what he thought was the correct door.

"Yes?"

The young woman who answered reminded him of the girl who'd stopped him on the sidewalk and asked him if he was okay the week before. She wasn't the same girl, but she reminded him of her. She sure didn't look like any Veda.

"Are you with the movers?" she asked.

"The movers," Jack repeated. He patted the spot to the left of his heart and smiled, happy to feel the comforting lump.

"The truck's arrived?" Her face lit up.

He nodded. Lately, Jack nodded at most things people said.

"Thank you, God. Finally." Her laugh was like silver bells. "Four days, four *days* without furniture. Don't let anyone tell you furniture isn't important."

"It's important all right."

"You don't look like a mover, in that jacket. You the supervisor?"

Jack nodded.

"Well, please send them up. Apartment 215. They know that, of course. Ooh, I can't wait."

Feeling that the young woman wanted him to check on some truck, Jack let his skipping legs carry his weight down the stairs. Just as he exited the building, a long semi with a globe of the world painted on its side heaved into view.

Two men jumped out of the cab and threw up the accordion door.

"Apartment 215," Jack said. "She'll be happy to see you guys."

"Sure, Pops," said the younger one, a guy with hair the color of a banana peel.

"You're the dad, huh. You can sign here," said the other guy, older, with a gray-flecked beard. Jack signed: John Galloway. He felt proud wielding the pen, as if she were his daughter, moving into her first apartment.

"Not the greatest neighborhood," the blond guy said.

Jack nodded. He'd see about that, make sure she knew to take precautions.

"This is so exciting," the girl said when he reappeared, following the movers who were hauling a sofa. He carried in a nightstand himself. Might as well help out. Moving into a new place when you're young— that struck him as a wonderful thing. The girl, Sarah, was training to be a nurse. This building was convenient to the hospital, and some other nurses lived here too, she assured him.

Jack patted his chest and looked up at the ceiling, thinking about how a woman named Veda also had access to this building, and thinking about the clients she attracted. "Change the locks," he told Sarah. "Never open the door to a stranger. You don't know who could be out there."

He carried up a few cardboard boxes from the truck. On his last trip, a guy who looked familiar passed him on the stairs, scrambling down. Langston.

It was this damned Alzheimer's thing. He'd gone to the wrong floor. Should've hit apartment 315, not 215. He puffed his way upward and gave the door a rat-a-tat. It opened. A strawberry blond gave him a look as narrow as his was large and frightening. "Veda?" he said.

"You're late, mister." She was running a brush through her hair with a ragged energy that announced she didn't care if it all fell out. "What's with you? Phil says you're good. Johnny-on-the-spot."

"Sorry." He patted the place below his shoulder. He felt like a kid tardy for class. "I had to help a friend. Moving day, ya know. I'm so sorry."

"Sure, sweetie." She shoved the brush into her purse and swiveled past him. "You can feed that story to Phil. He'll love it. But for me, this job's finished."

Jack whirled around as he glimpsed a bruise on her cheek. "That guy, he hurt you?"

She faced him, eyes slit narrower than before. "What else's new? Thanks for being such a Johnny-on-the-spot. Thanks. For nothing."

"I'll get him, next time," Jack called after her. "I promise."

"Won't be any next time for me," she threw over her shoulder. "Might not be one for you either."

That night he did manage to make it to rehearsal with the Civic Symphony. During the day he mostly felt confused, unfocused; but when it came to music, whether practicing alone or attending rehearsals, his mind cleared up.

"This music's hard," said Eric, his stand-mate—the guy who sat last, the one with no pinkie.

Jack shrugged his agreement as he rosined his bow. Next to what had happened that day, playing Mozart was a relief.

"I mean, Wenzel's nuts if he thinks we can play this." Eric barely moved his lips as he eyed the conductor. "Way over our heads. I'll never get it right in a million years."

"My mom would say, try your best." Jack set Mozart's overture to *The Marriage of Figaro* on the stand. "The better players cover us, anyway."

"I guess. That's the right attitude. I just wish I could play it." Eric wiggled the stub of his little finger.

Jack held up his left hand. "I got all my fingers, and I can't play it either. Me, I'm happy just to be here, in the middle of it all, even if I can't play the fast parts."

Eric tuned his A string. "That's a healthy way to look at it. You strike me as being patient, and wise." He gave Jack's owl eyes an appraising look. "We've shared this stand, two years now? I never asked—my guess is you're a counselor or something—but, if you don't mind the question, what do you do for a living?"

"Kill people." Jack gave the D string peg a downward twist, then turned it up to pitch.

Eric bent forward in a belly laugh that threatened his hernia.

"But only people who deserve it."

"You're a riot, Alice," Eric said.

"Alice? Alice who?"

"You know. You're my generation, aren't you? Alice Kramden. Jackie Gleason—Ralph Kramden. You know, how he was gonna send Alice to the moon?"

"Yeah. I remember." Jack's eyes grew even bigger behind the thick lenses. "I'm a security guard. That's what I meant. Work several neighborhoods."

"*Bang, bang.* You drop the bad guys." Eric wiggled the trigger finger of his bow hand. "You actually got a gun license with those eyes of yours?"

"I never miss a hit—a target." With regret, Jack recalled Langston. "Hardly ever." Good thing Eric was missing a pinkie and didn't know who he was talking to. Jack might have promoted him to the top of a hit list of his own.

When Jack returned home from rehearsal, three messages blinked on his answering machine. Phil sounded different, tight. He said to meet him at the Peacock Inn pool tomorrow, midmorning. Anything after ten was fine. "And don't forget to bring along your brain."

Jack's body sagged as he considered that last directive. Where exactly would he find it?

He walked into his bedroom and opened the nightstand drawer. His fingers rifled through pens and old scratched-up eyeglasses. Then he stopped. What was he looking for, anyway? His brain? The thing Phil suggested he bring along? Tired, he bounced down on the bed and fell asleep.

Next morning a new message blinked. "Don't forget. The Peacock. Ten sharp."

"Glad you reminded me," Jack said to the machine. It was already nine. He ate a bowl of Raisin Bran and headed out in his blue Bug. Didn't have to dress since he'd never taken off his clothes the night before. His rehearsal clothes, he called them. Gray knit pants with an elastic waistband and a dark-blue t-shirt, no collar. Collars got in the way of his violin's shoulder rest.

"What bed did you fall out of?" Phil asked at the sight of him.

Jack didn't answer. He couldn't remember falling out of any bed. He noticed that Phil was wearing nicely pressed slacks and one of his fancy sweaters, the gold crab pendant gleaming at his neck. He was in his usual lounge chair, sipping a margarita, a *People* magazine open on his lap.

"Seriously, why you dressed like that? You look like… I don't even know what you look like."

Jack said, "This is what I wear to rehearsal."

"Rehearsal. What rehearsal?"

"The Civic Symphony. We're playing *The Marriage of Figaro*. I play the violin."

"Oh, that violin crap. Sure, sure. You're the only terminator I know with a real violin in his case. Ha! Well, lookee here. This ain't no rehearsal. This is the real deal, and you blew it. Big time."

Jack remained standing, hands warm in the pockets of his knit pants. He looked at the pool's silky water. "Nobody's swimming," he said.

"Well, sure nobody's swimming. Pool's closed for the season. This dump's got no heat."

"But wasn't there a kid swimming just last week?" Jack tilted his chin upward as if the question was important.

"That fat little belly-buster? Yeah. So they closed the pool since then, to anybody who ain't nuts, that is. So what's your point?"

Jack couldn't say. Only that it felt good to remember something that far back. To have a lock on it. "So why are we out here?" Jack asked. "It's kind of cold out here."

"You're interviewing me, huh. Full of questions. So I like it out here. I like to sit around a pool. Always liked water. I like lounge chairs, and the sun, even if it's not always out. I like having some chick serve me a margarita poolside even if it ain't noon yet, and I'd like you to tell me what happened with Langston. And I don't wanna hear you left your gun in the car."

"I had my gun." Jack thought of taking the chair next to Phil's but hiked his shoulders instead, working to remember. Yeah, there was that girl who was moving in. He'd been concerned about her.

"Bravo. You brought your gun. Only Veda says you were like an hour late."

Jack remembered her bruised face. "Sorry about that."

"Sorry. Jack, my dear sweet Jack. You let me down twice in two weeks, and you never did that before in thirty years."

Jack gazed at the water, eyes slit. "I'm gonna get that guy," he said. "I promised Veda. He's a bad guy."

"That's the spirit. You gotta get him, get him today. Got that? I'm giving you his address, see? This'll be riskier, but we need him capped pronto. Park yourself outside that monster house of his, and when he comes out, *pow*. You know what he looks like, right?"

Jack took the card Phil held out to him. "Consider it done. For Veda."

Like a peeved hippo, Phil blew air through his lips. "Veda's out, ya know. Won't cooperate, so we have to go this riskier way."

Jack nodded, trying to comprehend the address on the card. The numbers and letters weren't making sense to him. It was like he'd never learned to read.

"You might say Veda's getting unruly. She's asking for more dough—for what you put her through, genius. I'm afraid she's going dangerous on us. Veda's beginning to make herself... inconvenient."

Inconvenient was one of Phil's code words. Even in his mental fog, Jack knew what that word meant.

"I know, I know. You won't cap a woman," Phil said.

"Except that once. I did that once."

"Mea culpa. Told you, that's on my headstone, not yours." Phil gave up on suppressing a laugh. "Pretty funny, you gotta say, how I got you thinking Mrs. Valencia was really a man in drag. That was before you got that thicker prescription. She was a looker, all right."

Jack pushed his glasses up onto his forehead and rubbed his eyes. "They had two kids. I remember asking you...'then how come they got two kids?'"

Phil downed the rest of his margarita. "Adopted. *Adopted*, I said. And what else? I said Valencia took his sweet time figuring out a few...oddities. Oh, Jacko boy, what you won't believe. But look, I had plenty of jokes played on me in my time. Plenty. Nothing to feel ashamed about. We can all be conned. I've been conned."

"She wasn't no man in drag."

"Maybe not, but to her husband—our client—well, she was a drag. Get it?" Phil's stomach jitterbugged beneath his baby-blue sweater. "But you know how it goes. We don't get to pick and choose these jobs. Like in the jungle, it's whatever comes your way. Or it's like a surgeon—which you are, as I told you; he operates on the good and the bad. Doesn't have a choice in the matter."

Jack gave his eyes a last rub, and let his glasses slide down onto his nose.

"You tired?" Phil asked. "Sure. Sure. You've had a time of it, with your mom and all. But this here's an emergency. There's a bonus in it for you too." He wagged his head. "Even though you screwed up those other two grand opportunities, I'm offering a double bonus— do the math—and uh, we're all a happy family again. Okay? This Langston, who you admit mussed up our friend Veda a bit more than could be called nice—this creep has to go. Today."

"A creep." Jack clasped his palms together, noticing, with gratitude, that he had two pinkies.

"You got the address."

Jack held up the card.

"You know what to do."

"Sure." But Jack wasn't actually all that sure where to go next. He asked, "Have I…have I been in this part of town before?"

"Sure you have. Back when Langston was still cool, he had us over to his place. Remember? That façade, like a fake mini-Italian villa. And that pool, big as a stadium out back? I loved that pool."

Jack nodded.

"Believe me. When you get there, everything will be familiar, and you'll know what to do."

Turning away from Phil, Jack patted the spot to the left of his heart. The bulge was missing. Nothing for it but to locate his car. Most likely the gun was waiting under the gray towel on the passenger seat.

And it was. He leaned into his VW and pulled the holster and gun over his head, snugging it under his arm. Then he walked around the block again. He thought he was lost, but the neon Peacock sign set him straight. Though unlit in daylight, it beckoned.

"What now, Jacko?" Phil tucked the *People* under his arm and rose from his chair. "Can't find your Rolls?

Jack looked at the sky, then at the sea-green lounge chairs scattered around the pool. Phil had assured him the place would look familiar when he arrived, and he'd know what to do. This place looked familiar enough, but also felt entirely foreign, just as the man with the gold crab pendant, spiking the sun into his eyes, seemed familiar and strange at the same time. His lips moved as if he was saying something. Jack, too busy to listen, scanned the territory as he always did on a job, checking its emptiness.

"I'm goin' in the lounge for a sandwich." Phil rolled the magazine in a tube and slapped it against his left palm. "And you—you better find your car, your gun, or your ass."

Phil's rubbery smile abruptly drooped as he caught sight of the gun in Jack's hand. His eyes flicked from the weapon to the magazine that he whipped open at the last moment, holding it up as if it were a shield. He croaked, "You're kiddin', right?"

Thwop, thwop.

Phil staggered backward, still gripping the *People*. He gazed at its cover longingly, as if hoping his demise might make a minor headline. Then came the splash. A back-buster.

Jack holstered the gun. That quick, he felt clearer in the head. Yeah, maybe this place was familiar after all, he thought as he strolled past lounge chairs and rubber tree plants to the parking lot. The kind of familiar that, with any luck, he'd never see again.

ELAINE MENGE, a native of New Orleans, lives in The Woodlands, Texas, with her husband and a stubborn, long-haired dachshund named Piccolo. Eleven of her suspense stories have appeared in *Alfred Hitchcock Mystery Magazine*, and another will come out this year in *Ellery Queen Mystery Magazine*. Her fiction has also appeared in several literary magazines, including *West Branch*, *Sou'wester*, and *Hawaii Review*. A graduate of the now-defunct Newcomb College of Tulane University, she received an MA in English literature from UNC-Chapel Hill, and an MFA. from LSU. She is a member of Mystery Writers of America.

Leftovers

David Steven Rappoport

MAINERS LOVE their boats. When winter comes they put them in dry dock and shrink-wrap them in white plastic. When summer approaches they rip off the wrap and put them back in the water.

It was early June in Horeb, population 2,421, a village on Merrymeeting Bay.

The village proper was tiny. Its main road—Massachusetts Street—ran about two miles from the Horeb exit on I-295 until it dead-ended into Water Road, aka Route 240, a small state highway. In between there were six streets that ran either perpendicular or parallel to Massachusetts. Horeb had one traffic light—flashing yellow—a gas station, a small general store, and a smaller diner. Woods and farms and former woods and farms made up the rest of Horeb's thirty-four square miles.

In the sixties, Horeb changed from a stolid farming community to a hippie carnival. In the years since the town had regained balance. Still, Horeb continued to be a rather eccentric place. It was now home to an array of cottage industries: weaving, soap making, organic lamb, pottery, heirloom vegetables, and handmade Windsor chairs. There was a town arts center that held exhibits of local painters and sculptors and housed an avant-garde theater company. Near it was an even more renegade establishment: the Maine Ephemera Museum. The museum sponsored exhibits of toothbrushes, paper clips, and painted flowerpots, and had a permanent collection of umbrella covers from around the world.

The weather was finally warm, and Electra Philemon—with the assistance of three local boys—was about to launch her employer's boat for the season.

Electra was a monumental woman in late-middle age, part Praxiteles and part bride of Frankenstein. She possessed more curves than a Greek island and a headful of frantic gray ringlets. She strode forcefully in her L.L.Bean boots across the acres of garden and muddy meadow that separated Ernestine Cutter's Georgian home from the bay. On its banks, Electra's employer, Deuteronomy Smelt, stored his trailered boat, an eighteen-foot 1974 Starcraft.

As she and her helpers approached, they noticed something unexpected: an increasingly foul smell. By the time they reached the boat, the smell was overwhelming.

"A fisher cat must have died in there," one of the boys suggested, referring to a nasty species of local weasel.

Electra sighed and nodded in agreement. "Boys, we ripping the plastic, then back to the house. I going for bleach, and we scrubbing the boat."

Vigorously, she began to rend the white plastic that covered the boat. The boys assisted.

It was only a matter of seconds before they saw the cause of the smell. Electra—who did not possess her given name for nothing—shrieked monumentally and then fell to her knees shaking her fists. The boys, exhibiting horror in its more subdued Yankee form, stood frozen.

"Who is that?" one of the boys finally asked, after peering at the swollen body.

"Don't know, but he looks wicked dead," the second said.

"I think we should call Officer Bernier," the third concluded, referring to the Sagadahoc county sheriff who lived in the village. The boy pulled a cell phone out of his pocket.

"Ask police if they bringing bleach," Electra suggested breathlessly between wails.

Ernestine Cutter, like most Horeb residents, knew that in recent years the dock and storage fees at the town marina had become too much for Deuteronomy. A good neighbor, Ernestine had graciously and tactfully allowed Deuteronomy to store the boat at her place.

Years earlier Deuteronomy had inherited money and a large old farmhouse from his aunt, Cornelia Smelt Merrill. She had married into a wealthy Maine family. What had been a substantial sum in 1975 had become microscopic by 2010. Deuteronomy was retired now. He'd penned thirty-six thrillers under the name Nash Hammer.

The first, *Spy Times Three*, had been published successfully in 1957. The last, *The Turban of Desire*, was quickly remaindered in 2001. His royalty checks, when they arrived, were hardly worth depositing.

Deuteronomy was more intelligent than talented, and more strategic than adaptable. The fifties and early sixties had served him well, as they were full of memes he understood: gin, Communism, prosperity, seduction. By the seventies, he was struggling but keeping up, substituting marijuana for martinis, adding computers to his espionage tool kit, and creating female characters with a diminished sense of moral order and extraordinarily large breasts.

By the 1990s, after the Cold War ended, the thrill had gone out of his thrillers. International terrorism, with its lack of nuance, held no interest for Deuteronomy. It had none of the vigor of Ernest Hemingway, the intrigue of Eric Ambler, the moral ambivalence of Graham Greene; even the testosterone of Mickey Spillane was missing. He was a man who understood thinking twenty moves ahead in a struggle with Russian espionage; he did not understand zealots blowing up the game board.

Electra had lived in Deuteronomy's house for years. She'd emigrated from Greece to the United States in the seventies to enter a lonely hearts marriage to a widower in Boston. The marriage turned out more *House of Atreus* than *House & Garden*, and Electra was pleased when her husband succumbed from natural causes on New Year's Eve 1978. She moved to Maine and worked as a maid in a hotel. Shortly after that she met Deuteronomy.

Deuteronomy's fourth wife had died almost eleven years earlier. He missed her. He rarely saw his daughter, who lived half a continent away. However, his granddaughter, Jezebel, had recently moved in. A recent graduate of Bowdoin College, with a double major in biology and French literature, she seemed unable to find a suitable job due to the Great Recession. So she had decided on medical school. She would become a gynecologist and work in French-speaking Africa. As Jezebel described her vision, "Madame Ovary, c'est moi."

Neither Electra nor Jezebel saw much of Deuteronomy, but then, no one did. Since his wife's death, he had gone out less and less. Finally, in the last few years, he emerged only at night, usually in the summer, to take midnight boat rides. Otherwise, unless it was essential, he saw no one and spoke to no one. He relied on Electra and Jezebel to manage all the practical elements of the household and his life. When communication was necessary, he often used postcards. There was no particular rationale for this idiosyncrasy—it was just what he did.

Deuteronomy spent his time in his bedroom, which was large and resembled an Edwardian men's club. Arts and Crafts wallpaper in morose shades of blue and green covered the walls, and navy-blue floor-to-ceiling velvet drapes blocked as much light and air as possible.

The room was furnished with a massive oak bed, several leather lounge chairs, a wall of books, and a large writing desk. On this sat his computer and a printer, both distrusted, but accepted as a part of the general cultural decline in which thoughtful men now found themselves. There was also an old hi-fi console, which Deuteronomy used to play classical records.

Most days passed uneventfully. He read, thought, wrote letters, or made notes for novels he would likely never write. At night he listened to music.

He was just about to emerge for breakfast when Electra, irate, burst into his bedroom. Fortunately he was already dressed in black slacks, a gray herringbone jacket, and a crisp white shirt with a striped bow tie.

"Dead body found in the boat. Is hidden in plastic wrap like leftover chicken!"

"What are you talking about?" Deuteronomy asked calmly.

"Maybe been in boat through winter: freeze and thaw, freeze and thaw, freeze and thaw," Electra continued, with sweeping, dramatic gestures evoking the rise and fall of the temperature. "Ugly! But him I know. Come to see you in the fall. Professor somebody."

"You don't mean Donald Laventhall?"

"Yes. This is the man. Laventhall."

"How was he killed? Stabbed? Shot? What?"

"I do not know this. No wound. No blood. But horrible!"

The door buzzer interrupted the conversation—an unusual occurrence in this household that had few visitors. Electra went to answer the door. Soon, Deuteronomy heard a male voice.

"The polices is here," Electra anxiously announced as she returned to his bedroom. "These polices they come to see you. I put them in parlor."

"I don't feel like seeing anyone," he replied.

"Is the polices!" Electra exclaimed vehemently.

"Yes. I suppose you're right," Deuteronomy said, rising dutifully to face the inevitable. He straightened his bow tie and walked down the hall.

A uniformed policeman sat on the sofa. The officer was perhaps forty, short, taut, and muscular. He carried a canvas bag, which he set on the floor. From it he removed a half-finished doily and went to work on it with a crochet hook.

"What are you doing there?" Deuteronomy asked.

"Tatting. Reduces stress," the officer replied gruffly. He continued his work as they spoke. "I'm Officer Bernier from the Sagadahoc county sheriff's office."

"I'm Deuteronomy Smelt. But you know that. I understand a man's body has been found in my boat."

"I'm afraid that's right. It appears he's been murdered."

"Have you identified him?"

"We think he is Donald Laventhall, a history professor who retired here from Boston. He lived alone and wasn't particularly social. None of his neighbors had seen him in months. They thought he might have gone to a warmer climate for the winter. Did you know him?"

"It's a small village. I've lived here all my life."

"So that's a yes? Were you and Mr. Laventhall friends?"

"I wouldn't say so."

"Your housekeeper told us he visited you."

"He wanted to talk about a project he was working on."

"And what was that?"

"A true crime book about the Cold War. He wanted to know what cases I thought he might include."

"Why would you know about that?"

"I used to write spy novels. My pen name was Nash Hammer."

"That's right. I think I knew that. Wasn't one of your books made into a movie?"

"Several were. There was a television series as well. That was years ago, of course."

The interview continued for another fifteen minutes: Who had access to the boat? When did he last use it? Did he know anyone who might have wanted to kill Donald Laventhall? Deuteronomy told Bernier all he knew, but it was very little. Bernier thanked him and left.

The next morning Jezebel rose slightly earlier than her usual noon and was in the kitchen baking when Electra appeared to cook Deuteronomy's lunch.

"What is you making?" Electra asked suspiciously.

"I'm experimenting with *madeleines*," Jezebel responded cheerfully, pronouncing the name in her flawless if affected Parisian accent. "It's a cookie in Proust."

Electra nodded, assuming this must be a new bakery in Portland.

The door buzzer sounded.

"Who is this?" Electra said.

"I suppose it must be the police again," Jezebel said breezily.

"You get door. I scrambling eggs."

Jezebel did as she was told and discovered an older man standing at the threshold. He was about Deuteronomy's age, tall, swarthy, and trim.

"Is Deuty at home?"

"Deuty? Do you mean Grand-père?"

"I used to work with him," the man continued. "That's what we called him: Deuty."

"You worked for his publisher?"

"No. In television. Though I am a fan of his books."

"They are fun, aren't they?"

"Is he at home?" the man asked again.

"I don't know if he's feeling sociable today. May I ask your name?"

"Tell him it's Radu Dubinky."

"I can't promise anything. Grand-père is quite the recluse. But come in if you like."

She escorted him to the parlor, and then walked down the hall to Deuteronomy's room and knocked gently on the door. "We have another visitor," she said casually. There was no response. She knocked again. "Grand-père?" Again there was no response.

Jezebel sighed with mild irritation and picked up a blank postcard from the random assortment piled on a table by the door. The card was from the fifties and read "Greetings from Rehoboth Beach." She took a pen from her pocket, wrote a brief note explaining that a guest had arrived, and slipped it under the door. She waited. A few moments later a reply postcard emerged: "On the World Famous Boardwalk, Atlantic City," which showed a pair of girls in wool bathing outfits. Jezebel read Deuteronomy's reply and returned to the parlor.

"My grandfather does not recognize your name. He wonders on what topic you wish to converse?" Jezebel said.

"We haven't seen each other in forty years. I worked on his television show. I've got to see him. I'm afraid it's urgent."

"I see. Why don't you just follow me? It'll save a lot of back and forth."

She led him to her grandfather's door and knocked again. "Grand-père, I have Mr. Dubinsky with me. He says he worked with you in television and that he must see you."

The man spoke through the door. "Deuty, it's Radu, Radu Dubinsky. I know you remember me, old buddy—I was the technical adviser on *Guns and Kisses*."

The door opened.

"I suppose you might as well come in," Deuteronomy said with some annoyance. "Thank you, Jezebel."

Deuteronomy shut the door. Radu studied the room. Deuteronomy studied Radu.

"Hello, Deuty. It's good to see you. Do you remember me?"

"More or less," Deuteronomy replied. "Please sit down," he continued, indicating one of the lounge chairs. He sat nearby in another. "As I'm sure you can imagine, I'm surprised to see you."

"I'm sure you are," Radu said. "The reason I'm here is that Donald Laventhall was my brother-in-law."

"Was he?" Deuteronomy responded, intrigued.

"My wife's brother. My wife and I live in New Hampshire. I'm retired now. She has family there."

"Did you think I might have more information? Or did you come because you thought I killed him?"

"Of course I don't believe you were involved. What possible motivation could you have? It's just that my wife's upset. She's very upset. I said I'd see if you knew anything. You see, the police don't seem to be getting anywhere and..."

"I can't help you," Deuteronomy said, interrupting. "I knew Don slightly. I saw him a few times last fall. He was writing a book about the Cold War. How did you find out it was my boat?"

"One of the police mentioned Don was found in Horeb. I thought I remembered you lived here. I still have a few old friends who can be helpful. One of them confirmed the boat was yours. So, you don't know anything?"

"I'm afraid not," Deuteronomy said. "Though I can't help but be intrigued that your brother-in-law's body just happened to end up in my boat." He smiled slightly. There was nothing he liked as much as speculation.

"In my day we would have considered that a dumb place to hide a body," Radu offered.

"Exactly. Thus, it appears that whoever put it there wanted it found and assumed it would be when the boat was unwrapped in the spring."

"That's plausible."

"Of course it is. But there are other questions. When one writes a thriller, critical pieces of evidence appear for one of two reasons: to inform or misinform. We know the body was placed to be found now. Why? Was it to mask the cause of death? The longer the body decomposed, the more difficult it would be to conduct a conclusive autopsy. Was it something else? The fact that the body was in my boat might imply a desire to get my attention or to implicate me in the crime. An alternate theory is that the discovery of Don's body could simply be a diversion, a way to throw people off something more important."

"That's as far as I got myself, more or less. Truth be told, I was just a CIA desk jockey. You, however, always had a great mind for these things. I thought you might have uncovered more."

"And here you are."

"Like I said, my wife's upset. So, what do you suggest we do now?" Radu asked.

"You tell me how wonderful it was to see me again. Then you drive home, tell your wife this trip was a waste of time, and wait for the police to do their job."

"So that's it? You don't know anything. You don't want to know anything. You're just going to leave it alone?"

After midnight, to avoid being observed, Radu and Deuteronomy walked a mile through the moonlit woods to Don's home. They carried a paper bag of supplies.

"I'm not sure about this," Radu said. "The police still have Don's house taped off."

"We'll just have a look around," Deuteronomy reassured him.

They continued to walk. Near their destination, Radu's foot caught on a tree root. He went flying to the ground, screaming an obscenity loudly as he did so. A light clicked on in a nearby house.

"Quiet, Radu. You're attracting attention."

Radu got up. They continued.

"There's a key by the back door," Radu said as they arrived at Don's house. "It's under the bottom step."

They gloved their hands, covered their shoes, took a flashlight from the bag, and approached the back door. It was covered with yellow crime scene tape. Radu hesitated.

"Come along," Deuteronomy said. "We'll make it look like raccoons broke in." They went in through an unlocked window.

The police had already done a thorough job of searching the house. Whatever there may have been that explained anything was no longer there. Giving up on the inside of the house, they exited through the window. That's when Deuteronomy spotted something of interest at the side of the house: a pile of stuffed black-plastic trash bags. "Bring the flashlight over here."

Radu held the light while Deuteronomy opened a bag and began pawing through it.

Initially the trash yielded nothing but trash: envelopes, bills, tissues, and other detritus. Then Deuteronomy saw something of possible interest: a rectangular plastic container full of a fetid substance. He examined the label: TRADITIONAL BULGARIAN STYLE SHEEP FETA. It came from a local producer, Omurtag Farms.

"That's odd," Deuteronomy said. "Don't you think?"

"Why do you say that?"

"Don was allergic to dairy products," Deuteronomy explained. "Profoundly allergic. Electra offered him lamb with tzatziki when he visited, and he wouldn't eat it. Why would he have cheese in his refrigerator?"

"That's right. I forgot he was allergic."

Suddenly there were headlights nearby and a rapidly approaching police siren. Without another word Radu jumped up and ran into the woods. Deuteronomy hesitated a moment, then also started to run. Unfortunately, it was too late: he was caught in a high-beam flashlight.

A few minutes later Deuteronomy found himself handcuffed and in the back of Officer Bernier's car. He'd been arrested for trespassing. Deuteronomy spent the rest of the night in a cell.

In the morning Jezebel bailed him out. Deuteronomy went home, took a shower, changed, and went out again.

He drove to Omurtag Farms, which was located on the edge of Horeb. Its brightly painted sign announced that it was both "organic" and "biodynamic."

The gate was open, and Deuteronomy drove through. He continued down a winding dirt road about a quarter of a mile. He arrived at a series of connected, whitewashed buildings in a little house, big house, back house, barn configuration, typical to old New England homes.

Deuteronomy parked near the barn and got out. He saw a young woman feeding chickens in a large enclosure and approached her.

"I wonder if you can help me. I'm here to make an inquiry about someone who may have purchased your feta cheese."

"You'll need to talk to Anastas. He should be in the dairy barn." She pointed to a large outbuilding a few acres away.

Inside the barn, Deuteronomy found a swarthy man of middling age and height. He wore a t-shirt that read HOREB, TICK CAPITAL OF THE WORLD. His shoulder-length, salt-and-pepper hair and an unkempt beard that descended to his stomach completed the picture.

"Are you Anastas?"

"Yes," he said, with a significant accent that was difficult to identify.

"I can't place your accent."

"Bulgaria."

"Really? How did you end up in New England?"

"I fall in love with *Moby Dick*, then I find out nobody hunts the whales no more. Meanwhile, I emigrate."

"I see," Deuteronomy continued. "I'm here about your feta cheese. Actually, about someone who was one of your customers. Do you remember a man named Donald Laventhall? Here's his picture," he said, displaying an image he'd cut out of the Brunswick *Times Record*, the daily newspaper of the nearest town of any size to Horeb.

"I know this name. Why is this?"

"He's dead. His body was discovered a few days ago."

"Why do you ask about this man? He die from our cheese?"

"No, although I suppose if he had it would have been a *feta accompli*," Deuteronomy said, unable to resist himself. "I'm merely trying to learn all I can about him."

Anastas thought for a moment. "I do not recall him. You can ask my wife."

"Where would I find her?"

"We have little store in front. I take you."

They walked to the main building and went in through a side door. Inside, in what was once a barn, there were refrigerator and freezer cases of products for sale, along with bins of seasonal vegetables. Deuteronomy glanced inside one of the cases and found several varieties of cheese.

A woman who looked remarkably similar to Anastas minus the beard sat on a stool beside a cash register.

"Galina," Anastas said, "this man is here about man found dead."

"Do you remember Donald Laventhall?" Deuteronomy asked her. He showed her the newspaper photograph.

"Yes, I know him. He is here once or twice. He ask lots of questions," Galina replied. "This is what I tell the other man."

"Someone else was here asking about Donald Laventhall?"

"Yesterday. A tall man. Older. Dark." It sounded like Radu.

"Thank you for your time," Deuteronomy said, moving toward the door. Before he could reach it, it opened.

A tall, thin man came in. He was in his sixties, had bright carmine hair, a wildly tie-dyed t-shirt, and pink-and-white stripe sunglasses. He was Howard Oliver, a local artist and proprietor of the Maine Ephemera Museum.

"Deuteronomy," Howard said with some surprise, "how nice to see you out and about!"

"Good morning, Howard," Deuteronomy said flatly. He didn't like effusive people.

"Anastas. Galina. Don't you look well!" Howard said, greeting them. "I was thrilled you phoned!"

"I get what you came for," Galina said, disappearing into another room. Moments later she reappeared with three proletarian umbrellas covered in the usual Stalinist color palette: drab and dingy. She handed them to Howard and said with pride, "My sister send these from Romania just to put in the museum."

"What a gift! What a gift!" Howard effused, taking the objects. "Along with the umbrellas your brother sent from Russia, Ukraine, and Georgia, and your other sister sent from Bulgaria, our Eastern European umbrella cover collection will be world-class!"

Deuteronomy took a detour on his drive home and visited the public library in Brunswick.

"Do you have a telephone directory for Los Angeles?" Deuteronomy asked the librarian.

"We don't keep those anymore. The information is online now."

"Can you help me retrieve a Beverly Hills phone number?" Deuteronomy asked. "And after that I'd like to check on a man from Eastern Europe."

"Are you seeking his phone number as well?"

"No. I'm looking for his obituary."

That evening Deuteronomy called Frank Shapiro's home in Beverly Hills. Frank had produced *Guns and Kisses*. After a few minutes of pleasantries—always difficult for Deuteronomy, who didn't understand why people seemed to enjoy small talk—he brought up the subject of Radu Dubinsky.

"My memory isn't what it used to be. Maybe yours is better. You remember the guy, don't you?" Deuteronomy asked.

"Yeah. Some actor. Used a made-up name and said he'd been in military intelligence in Vietnam."

"Right. It was all bullshit. He was just an actor," Deuteronomy confirmed. "I also remember that you said you admired his pluck, so you fired him as technical adviser but gave him a small recurring role on the show. Am I remembering that correctly?" Deuteronomy asked.

"I remember that's what I told you."

"What do you mean?"

"I mean that I hate liars, and I wanted to fire the son-of-a-bitch. The network wouldn't let me. They insisted that I keep him on. They also insisted I keep it quiet."

"Why would the network do that?"

"I have no idea. The son of a bitch got in my hair for a couple of months—insisted on script revisions, that kind of thing—then he disappeared. I tried not to get paranoid about it."

"So he wasn't just an out-of-work actor?"

"I don't know. Why are you asking about this after all this time?"

"No reason. It just crossed my mind. Thanks, Frank."

A few hours later a great commotion woke Deuteronomy and everyone else in the house. They went outside and saw the Horeb volunteer fire department, and the volunteer firemen from three surrounding communities, rushing toward the Maine Ephemera Museum. The museum was blazing, creating a glow that lit up the village. The fire went on the rest of the night. By morning the fire was out, and the building was nothing more than memories and ashes.

Deuteronomy had watched the blaze for a long time. Shortly after dawn he'd gone back into the house and made some coffee. He sipped it thoughtfully. A few hours later he decided to visit Officer Bernier.

"The day before yesterday I received a visit from Radu Dubinsky, a man I knew four decades ago and hadn't seen since," Deuteronomy began, after seating himself in Bernier's office. "He told me he was Donald Laventhall's brother-in-law."

"And?" Bernier said, picking up his crochet hook.

"It's complicated, but I thought he was lying. I called somebody I know to verify my memory of some key facts. It's not clear who this man is now—or who he was forty years ago. He may or may not be Donald Laventhall's brother-in-law. But there is something that seems critical: Donald Laventhall was writing a book about unsolved cases from the Cold War."

"Go on."

"I found Bulgarian cheese in Don's trash. He didn't eat dairy products; he was allergic. It was odd, so I followed up. Don had visited the farm that produced the cheese. I think he learned something there that got him killed."

"And what could that possibly have been?" Bernier said, with more than a hint of sarcasm.

"There was a famous unsolved Cold War assassination case," Deuteronomy continued. "The victim was a Bulgarian writer named Gregori Markov. He defected to the West in the late sixties.

"The Communists made three attempts to kill him. They finally succeeded in September of 1978. Markov was waiting at a London bus stop when he felt a slight pain—like an insect bite—on the back of his right thigh. He said that he turned around and saw a man pick up an umbrella off the ground and scurry across the street. The man got into a taxi and drove off. Markov died a few days later."

"What does this have to do with Laventhall?" Bernier asked impatiently.

"I'm getting to that. An autopsy revealed that the cause of death was ricin, an extremely toxic poison. It was injected into Markov's thigh in a tiny metal pellet. The ricin was likely delivered through a small injection gun embedded in that umbrella. Of course, no one's ever proved that, and the umbrella's never been recovered."

"I still don't get it," Bernier said.

"Yesterday I learned a woman has been giving umbrellas from Eastern Europe to Howard Oliver. The fire last night was arson, wasn't it?"

"It might have been."

"I think the umbrella that killed Gregori Markov somehow ended up in the Ephemera Museum. It was an unfortunate leftover of the Cold War, a nasty loose end. Don somehow found out it was in the museum and was going to write about it. That's why the guy that visited me, Dubinsky, killed him. Then he burned down the museum last night to get rid of the umbrella."

"Fanciful as it is, none of that explains why Don's body was in your boat."

"That was a ruse, likely carried out by Radu. The idea was inspired by one of my books, *Cat and Spouse*. The villain plants a body in a rowboat as a diversion. A husband-and-wife spy team finds the body, but they realize there's much more going on. Eventually they uncover a plot to blow up the Hermitage. One of the galleries hides an underground vault in which smuggled US military documents are hidden."

"That sounds like a James Bond movie."

"It was made into a movie. Unfortunately, it didn't involve 007—or anything else of interest." Deuteronomy sighed. "It was directed by a pompous *auteur* on psychedelic drugs just out of UCLA film school. Mercifully, it was only released to drive-ins in the Midwest."

Bernier chuckled. "I think you've just described a great plot for your next book. Go home and write it, and let me get back to work."

Later in the day Deuteronomy received an unexpected phone call from Officer Bernier. Mumbling sheepishly, he announced that he had received some sort of visit—he wouldn't say from whom. The trespassing charges had been dropped. Deuteronomy was no longer under suspicion for Donald's murder. There was no forensic evidence linking him to the body. Further, in Bernier's words, "No murderer could make up something that ridiculous to create an alibi."

"And what about the fire?" Deuteronomy asked.

"What about it?" Bernier responded, in a tone of discomfort just palpable enough to suggest the investigation might not be moving forward.

Deuteronomy walked home. A block away, he saw a man who appeared to be Radu Dubinsky walking in the other direction. He was carrying something.

"Radu!" Deuteronomy called after him.

Radu did not stop. Instead, he began to run. Deuteronomy accelerated, but Radu moved much faster. He reached his car and sped away before Deuteronomy could catch up or even read the license plate. In the process, Radu dropped what he was carrying.

Deuteronomy picked it up. It was a paper plate of cookies covered in plastic wrap.

"Do you remember Radu, the man who visited a few days ago? Did he visit again?" Deuteronomy asked Electra, who was in the kitchen washing dishes.

"I do not see nobody. I am here cleaning up. Jezebel make more pastries," Electra said, indicating a platter of *madeleines*.

"Where is Jezebel?"

"Taking a bath."

Deuteronomy put down the plate he had brought in with him. It also held *madeleines* or at least what remained of them after they were dropped. He walked up the stairs.

The door to Jezebel's room was open. He went in. Quickly, he scanned the surfaces and then checked the drawers. Finally, he opened the closet.

Inside, on the floor, he found a plastic bag with a can of acetone and several rags.

Jezebel appeared wrapped in a towel.

"Are you looking for something?"

"I thought a shirt of mine had ended up in here," Deuteronomy said.

"I have wonderful news," Jezebel exclaimed. "I've been offered a full scholarship to medical school in Washington, DC. I start in the fall."

"Was that the deal?"

"What do you mean?"

He opened the closet door again and took out the bag. He held it up, displaying it to Jezebel.

She looked at it for a moment, then shrugged. "That's history," she said. "There is nothing more to be said about anything that's happened. Now, if you don't mind, Grand-père, I would like to get dressed."

"Do that. And when you're done, pack your things."

Deuteronomy went downstairs. He closed his bedroom door and locked it, then he put the *St. Matthew Passion* on the hi-fi. He sat in his favorite leather chair and disappeared into the mathematical certainty of Bach.

AUTHOR

DAVID STEVEN RAPPOPORT (davidstevenrappoport.com) is a former playwright (two plays Off-Broadway, as well as TV and radio). His mystery novel *Husbands and Lap Dogs Breathe Their Last* will be published soon by Mainly Murder Press. David lives in Chicago.

CPSIA information can be obtained
at www.ICGtesting.com
Printed in the USA
FFOW03n1442191215
19594FF